ROGUE

LAURA MARIE
ALTOM

Rogue

Copyright © January 2016 by Laura Marie Altom

SEAL Team: Disavowed series

To become a United States Navy SEAL, a man must be physically forged in steel and able to mentally compute life or death situations with laser accuracy and speed. Our country trusts these men with the most sensitive military operations—many so covert that once they are successfully completed, they are never spoken of again.

This series celebrates one particularly fierce band of brothers who valiantly battled terrorists whose crimes against nature and humanity were far too great to chance escape. On a dark night, on foreign soil, SEAL Team Alpha witnessed acts so unspeakably cruel against women, infants and small children that their consciences would not allow anything other than their own brand of justice for the scum terrorist cell.

A trial would have been too good for these pigs, and so, one-by-one they were taken out, and the women and children they'd used were freed. By dawn, an entire region breathed easier. The men of Alpha found themselves heroes to those whose lives they had saved, but virtual criminals in the eyes of the organization they served. After a lengthy investigation, their elite, covert team was formally disbanded.

They now spend their lives deep undercover, still serving—no longer their country, but individuals who find themselves in need of not only their own personal warrior, but a particular brand of justice.

While honorably discharged, these men and their actions will forever be *disavowed* . . .

SEAL Team: Disavowed series

1

*O*ne wrong move.

That's all it would take for Maisey and her unborn child to die.

For disavowed Navy SEAL Nash Adamson, Maisey represented his first crush, his first kiss. His first *everything*. They could have had it all—until she'd dumped him. Now that fate had forced their reunion, they not only had years between them, but his dead wife and son.

The irony of the situation hadn't escaped him.

In and out, he chanted in his head with each breath. He'd make this an in-and-out mission, then never see her again.

Through his NVG's alien-green light, Nash counted ten of her husband's thugs guarding the south Florida compound's west border. The Everglades were isolated, but this place was located on a remote island among hundreds of islands. Even with satellite maps and photos and state of the art GPS, it had taken Nash hours by boat to reach it.

As a SEAL—make that *ex*-SEAL—he might have been trained to deal with all manner of chaos, but he was also smart enough not to rely on miracles. Rather than fighting what was sure to be an overwhelming show of force, he realized his best course of action was stealth.

The single-story, sprawling Spanish style home might be remote, but a fortress it was not. The stucco exterior featured plenty of easily accessible windows and balconies with handy-dandy, climbable trellises. The roof was tile, and sloped low enough to run across in a pinch.

In short, Maisey's hubby, drug kingpin Vicente Rodriguez, was a dumbass.

Still—even a dumbass could get Maisey or Nash's ass killed.

Above Nash's steady pulse sang the nighttime swamp. The hum of insects. The bellow of bullfrogs and the occasional grunt of a gator. The place had more bio-danger per square inch than anywhere else he'd recently traveled. Sure, the Amazon basin had the *Sunshine State* beat, but not by much. Escaping Maisey's sicko hubby was only half the battle. He'd then have plenty of slimy, hissing, biting obstacles to circumvent to ensure their safety.

Once he'd established a rhythm to the perimeter guards' flow, Nash eased through shadows to the compound's weakest link—its electrical box that was linked to a generator. The security system was surprisingly rudimentary. Took mere moments to rewire.

The early August day had been a scorcher.

Crouched against a still-warm brick wall, he flipped up his goggles, giving his eyes time to adjust before using a retractable mirror to peer into the window above. Three goons lounged around a kitchen table, M16s resting alongside steaming coffee and Danish.

Nice domestic scene.

Research told Nash that Vicente was one of the region's most lucrative dealers. Miami authorities had had him on their radar for years, but when it came to maintaining his squeaky clean image, the guy was a master. Not only was he suspected of buying off every local police force within a hundred miles, he'd wooed locals with perks like college scholarships for underprivileged youth and new public pools, clinics and baseball fields. Did Maisey know he already had a nice, Catholic *wifey* tucked away in his Columbian palace? The fact that Nash could possibly be the one telling her made him sick. Her mom had been the one to alert him that she was in trouble.

Satellite photos had given Nash a blueprint to

follow. A quick check of the laminated diagram he'd stashed in a pocket reminded him to hug this wall to a ninety degree turn, at which point he'd find a courtyard with a pool framed by six bedrooms. The trick would be finding the one housing Maisey.

Lucky him, lights were out behind all but one set of French doors.

The lone illuminated room had open curtains.

Lying on a floral spread, looking fourteen-months pregnant was Maisey. If she hadn't sported tear-stained cheeks and cuffed hands clasped over her belly, he might have thought her at peace. Her blond curls were as unruly as ever and her petite frame made her appear all the more vulnerable.

Throat unexpectedly tight, he fought a nostalgic rush—not only memories of good times shared, but the agonizing finality of learning his pregnant wife's fate.

Thirty yards behind him, a twig snapped.

He froze, then ducked behind the pool equip-ment shed to wait for a two-man guard team to pass. The guy nearest him smoked. The acrid scent warred with the swamp's mossy, fungal smells.

The pool pump kicked on.

Once the men passed, Nash used the noise to his advantage, masking his steps across the pea grav-el pool surround.

With Maisey's room exposed, he entered the house through one of the darkened rooms. She'd understandably be happy to see him, but he couldn't risk that scene being played out in front of her guards.

The French door's lock was easy enough to pick.

Inside, the artificially-cooled air hit him like a wall. It took a moment to adjust after the swamp's stifling heat. Nash assumed the dark space would be empty—wrong. The courtyard's dim lights showed an off-duty goon stretched across the bed, his black fatigues and boots out of place on the floral spread.

Holding his breath, Nash crept to the door, eking it open. Once his vision adjusted to the brightly lit hall, he searched for signs of life.

Finding no one, he turned left, reining in his hammering pulse. He'd been on far more dicey missions, yet this was personal. In an odd twist of fate, he'd been given the opportunity to save his wife and unborn child all over again and he wouldn't let them down.

Only, you already did.

Nash squashed the negative voice in his head to focus on how to best approach Maisey without inducing an emotional show. He had to keep her cool. He couldn't risk her alerting guards within her view.

Holding his breath, he entered what for all practical purposes was Maisey's *cell*.

She appeared to be sleeping, but taking no chances, he kept to the room's edge. If he shut the curtains before she woke, he could privately brief her on the escape plan. Otherwise, to assure they had no audience, he'd duck behind her bed.

Three feet from his goal, she bolted upright. "Who are you?"

"Mais," he whispered, removing his combat helmet, "it's me—Nash."

"Who?" Narrowed pale blue eyes spoke of her confusion. "*Nash*? From high school? You work for Vicente?"

"No. Your mom asked me to find you."

His peripheral vision caught a glint from outside. If Vicente's men caught him now, he'd be in a shitstorm. Ducking beside a dresser, he put his finger to his lips. "Don't look at me. I'm not here."

Not only did she not follow his instructions, she waved toward whoever was outside.

"Knock it off," he ground from between clenched teeth. "What's wrong with you?"

"You have to leave or Vicente will kill us both."

"*Leave*?" He shook his head. "Woman, I'm here to rescue you."

A knock sounded on the French door. A muffled voice asked from outside, "Miss Maisey, you okay?"

Mouth dry, Nash readied his Glock for action.

"I-I'm fine," she called. In an awkward scoot from the bed, she approached the drapery, then jerked it shut. "Thanks for checking in."

Nash took the luxury of exhaling, then lit into

6

her. "What the hell's wrong with you? You're treating your jailers like friends."

"I have no choice." Seated on an upholstered side chair, she hugged her hands to her belly, whispering, "Vicente made it clear. Either I play by his rules, or he'll kill me." Voice trembling, she said, "I-I saw him shoot a supposed friend—a man we'd shared meals with—in the head. For my baby's sake, I have to do as he says. More than anything, he wants a son. He won't hurt me as long as I'm carrying his child."

"Key words . . ." Kneeling in front of her, Nash searched for the right message to make her see reason. "*As long as you're carrying his baby*, you're safe. What happens after your son's delivery? Do you honestly think, having witnessed Vicente murder on a whim, he'll keep you around?" He gestured to her cuffed hands. "He's restrained the mother of his child. Who does that?"

"I know." Her expression clouded. Tears pooled in her eyes. "I'm in a bad spot, but I have to trust that everything's going to be okay."

Rocking back on his heels, Nash closed his eyes and groaned. "This is the most busted-ass rescue mission ever. Any second, Vicente's goons could rush in here, killing us both, and you're in a unicorn and rainbow fog. *Wake up, Maisey.* We've got to get out of here—*now*."

Her soft cries only steeled his resolve.

"No time for tears. Sorry your marriage went bad. But—"

"We're n-not even married. H-he lied to me. He already h-has a wife, but she's in Columbia. She can't have children, but he told me he'll never divorce her because of his faith." Her once light tears were now borderline hysterics. "*His* faith! What about mine? A-all my life I've struggled to be good, yet here I am, the unwed mother of a drug lord's b-baby."

Nash should've reached out to Maisey, drawing her into a hug while whispering sweet assurances into her hair, but he was no longer capable of that level of compassion. Losing his wife and son had changed him. Steeled him. Now, he was a machine calibrated to one goal—keeping this woman safe.

"Get your act together." Grasping her wrists, he made quick work of popping the locks on her cuffs. "Sixty seconds, we're ghosts."

"I can't," she said on the heels of a wail. "Where would we even go?"

"Trust me. I've got a plan." Nash rose to his full height, and slapped his helmet back on. "I don't mean to be cruel, but wise up and realize Hubby views you as nothing more than his own personal incubator, which is why we've got to bounce."

He scooped her into his arms.

"Put me down!" Bucking against his hold, she made it a nightmare for Nash to kill the room's overhead lights, then gauge between a crack in the drapes if their *friends* were within eyeshot. "You don't know what you're doing. Vicente will kill us both."

"No biggee . . ." Jaw clenched, Nash forced a breath before opening the door leading to the hall. "If you don't stop fighting me, we're already dead."

2

Maisey Blake bucked and kicked and did every-thing within her power to escape Nash's bind-ing hold. The one thing she didn't do was scream. Why? The last thing she wanted was to attract atten-tion. What didn't Nash get about the fact that as long as she was pregnant, she held all the power? As soon as she went into labor, Vicente would get her and their son safely to a hospital. Once there, she'd solicit help. While she adored her mother for send-ing out her own personal cavalry, if Vicente or one of his men caught her trying to escape, there would only be more trouble.

"Stop fighting," Nash demanded.

"I will if you put me down. I have a plan for af-ter the baby's born. I know I can get Vicente to see reason and let me share in raising our son."

"What happened to you, Mais?" Nash kept right on charging down the endless corridor. He passed a light switch and flicked it off. "Back when I knew you, you weren't this clueless."

She struggled all the harder, writhing to pummel his chest. "Put me down!"

"Hey!" called a voice from the dark. Maisey winced against the sudden glare of lights.

"Miss Maisey?" The guard sounded confused.

"Boss told me we're moving her," Nash said in an authoritative tone.

"I haven't heard. Mr. Rodriguez briefs everyone regarding his woman." Eyes narrowed, he asked, "Who are you?"

"Set me down." Throughout the exchange, Maisey's heart beat faster. Afraid runaway blood pressure could harm her baby, she tugged Nash's sleeve. "I'm fine walking on my own."

"Sure?" The warmth in his voice feigned concern. In reality, if Nash cared one iota, he would never have interfered in her business. All the same, he set her to her feet, never loosening his hold on her upper arm.

"Both of you stay put." The guard took a walkie-talkie from his belt. "Mr. Rodriguez, this is Manuel. I've got a situation with Miss Maisey. I need to verify you gave the okay for her transport?"

"Negative," said Vicente, his voice tinny over

the radio. "Shoot to kill whoever she's with and disable her—just don't aim for my child."

In the moment it took Maisey to grasp the fact that the man she'd once loved had ordered his associate to hurt her, any illusions she might have had for her pregnancy to have a happy ending were shattered.

Nash was right.

She'd been a fool in not doing everything in her power to escape.

"*Run!*" Nash delivered two blows to the guard, dropping him to his knees. After taking the injured man's weapon, Nash steered Maisey into the night.

"Shoot her!" The booming voice unmistakably belonged to the man she'd once believed to be her husband. "Aim for her legs! Don't hurt my son!"

"I'll cover," Nash pushed her ahead. "Get out that side door. I'm right behind you."

Gunfire erupted.

This time, she didn't question his orders. Why hadn't she listened before? If she'd left peacefully, it might have been hours before anyone had noticed she'd gone.

She wrenched open the deadbolt, then darted into the dark, muggy night. Thick air gripped her as tightly as her fear, making it hard to think or breathe. As Nash had directed, she should have kept moving, but where would she even go?

Bullets exploded against the lawn where she

stood, forcing her to run blindly. She wore a flimsy nightgown and slippers. Dirt hit her exposed arms and cheeks with such force she couldn't be sure whether or not she'd been shot.

"Hurry!" Fingers once again digging into her upper arm, Nash propelled her off of the manicured lawn and into the swamp. Vines tangled about her feet and thorns clawed her hands. Warm mud oozed into the soles of thin satin house shoes. "Faster!"

"I'm trying," she snapped, barely able to catch her breath. Pulse racing, love for her baby propelled her ever deeper into the night. As much as she tried telling herself this could only be a nightmare from which she'd soon wake, the continued *pop* of gunshots shattered all illusion, drumming into her head their horrifying reality.

"I-I can't do this," she cried, on the verge of throwing up. Though this was hardly the time for a hormonal breakdown, once tears started they refused to stop.

"Yes, you can."

When she slowed, Nash hefted her into his arms, somehow impossibly still trudging forward through mud and riotous vegetation.

The gunshots had stopped, but Vicente's bark carried on the thick, moldy-smelling air. *Find her!*

"We'll never escape him," Maisey cried against Nash's chest. "He'll never give up."

13

"Neither will we."

He carried her for what she guessed was another fifteen minutes before they came to a clearing and a small, sandy beach.

"Son of a . . ." After setting her down, he flicked on a light on his helmet to inspect a section of rope tied to a cypress. "Looks like it's been cut. See how clean the break is? The markings in the sand?"

"Yes." By faint moonlight, she noticed footprints and a wide indentation where it looked as if something heavy had been dragged.

"Looks like *Hubby's* friends circled around us, and helped themselves to our ride. Not sure why they didn't just wait for us to show up, but I'm not complaining."

"Don't call him that."

"Huh?" He cocked his head.

"Vicente. Don't refer to him as my husband. And what does any of this mean?" She gestured to the disturbed sand. "You have another plan, right?"

He sighed. "Sure. Assuming we reach that boat before they do."

3

Hours later, when Nash no longer heard the shouts of Vicente's men, he gave himself permission to stop.

Though cloaked in hundred percent humidity and heat, Maisey's teeth chattered. Shock? From a basic first aid kit he carried in one of many pockets on his black cargo pants, he took a metallic survival wrap. Wouldn't do as much for her as a nice fire, but at least it'd keep her from losing additional body heat. As for that fire, he couldn't take the risk of smoke leading Vicente's men right to them.

"T-thank you," she managed through her latest violent shiver.

"No problem." He'd set her at the base of a cypress. Moonlight did nothing to sugarcoat the toll their *adventure* had already taken. For him, what they'd been through was all in a day's work—physically easier than some of the missions he'd had to endure. For her, with her delicate features dirt-smudged, blond curls laced with leaves and small vines, shoulders sagging in defeat, she wore the dull-eyed mask of hopelessness he'd often seen on refugees.

While his training told him to secure their perimeter with booby traps designed to give a few precious seconds notice in case they were found, he couldn't in good conscience leave his pregnant friend alone and shivering.

"You gotta relax." Seated alongside her, he pulled her against him, intent on sharing his warmth. "We've got this."

As if operating on instinct, she snuggled closer. Leaning into him with what little remained of her strength.

For the first time in forever, he felt every inch a protector. Ironic that he was feeling now. It was his inability to feel that had his teammates worried. His friend and business partner, Harding, had forced him to take some time off, told him to get his shit together. The pain of losing his wife and son had been indescribable. So bad that he'd found it best to construct a wall around that part of his life, compartmentalizing it in a corner of his heart that would never again see daylight.

When Maisey stopped shivering, Nash reached into another pocket for a protein bar. "Eat."

She took it, but asked, "What about you?"

"I'm good. There's more. Plus, come daylight, I'll go shopping."

"Shopping?" She lifted her brows.

"Guess scrounging might be a better word. There's plenty of food out here. We just have to find it."

"Please," holding the bar in front of his mouth, she urged, "you have some, too. I don't feel right hogging it all for myself."

To get her off his case, he bit a corner, then pushed it away. "Happy?"

"You always were stubborn."

True. His tenacity served him well. The only thing he'd ever given up on was his love for this woman.

Having chewed the last bite of her mini-meal, she said, "You told me my mom sent you. How did she know where I was? For her own safety, I begged her to stay out of my business."

"You and your mom used to be tight. What happened that you wouldn't ask her for help?"

She took a long time answering. "Vicente. From the first time I mentioned him, her warning bells rang. She had no trouble advising me to stay away."

Maisey had stopped shivering. Wanting to keep her talking, to keep her mind from their less than

17

ideal location and situation, Nash asked, "Why didn't you see the same signs?"

"I wanted the fairy tale. For the first time in my life, I felt special. This man made me feel like I was the most amazing woman in the world."

"Thanks." Her comment struck like a sucker punch. Didn't matter that it'd been almost a decade since their last kiss, or that he'd already found and lost his wife, Maisey's long ago rejection still stung. "Good to know how much you cared."

"Really?" she asked with a put upon sigh. "We hadn't even graduated high school. Did you honestly, for one second, think I'd marry you? Signing on for a lonely life of living on some remote Navy base while you were off getting yourself killed? Or worse—behaving like my father? No, thanks."

He forced a chuckle. "Let me get this straight, life with me would've been worse than a sham marriage to a drug lord?"

Covering her face with her hands, she shook her head. "That's not at all what I mean, you're mixing—"

"Don't move . . ." A long, dark rope slithered from their tree.

4

"Freeze . . ."

"What? Why?" She started to look over her shoulder, but Nash slowly reached for a mean-looking knife. Forehead furrowed, his narrowed eyes and pressed lips told her he wasn't fooling.

"Don't. Move. An inch."

Palms sweating, pulse racing, Maisey wasn't sure her heart could take much more.

"No matter what . . . stay still."

Afraid to even nod, she swallowed hard, assuming Nash knew she understood.

Painstakingly slow, he raised his arm, menacing knife held at the ready. Drawing his lower lip into his mouth, he inched closer, and then lunged, swinging at whatever was behind her with such force she heard his knife's swoosh alongside her ear.

When that *something* thumped against her back, she screamed, scrambling to her feet with newfound superhuman strength.

Writhing on the dirt were two halves of a cottonmouth.

Growing up in Florida, she'd been schooled on which snakes to steer clear of and this one topped the list.

Hands clutched to her chest, she couldn't breathe past the wall of panic rising in her throat. Would this night ever end? The man she'd loved ordered thugs to shoot her, and now she faced venomous snakes?

"What are you doing?" she asked.

Nash had sliced off the snake's head and was now stripping the skin. "Making breakfast."

She retched.

"You might feel that way now," he said with a chuckle, "but pardon the rhyme—the meat is sweet. It'd really be good deep-fried with beer batter, but we'll have to make do."

"You're crazy. Get me out of here."

"That's the plan." He used a small stick to spear the snake lengthwise like on a spit. "But last I checked my GPS, we're off course by a good five miles."

"So you *do* have somewhere specific in mind for us to be?"

"Yeah." He gathered brush and small twigs, dropping them onto a pile. "And if you hadn't fought me back at Hubby's—sorry, Vicente's—you'd have already been home in a nice, soft bed."

Legs too rubbery from the snake incident to stand, Maisey crumpled to her former nest against the tree. Before leaning back, she glanced up and found the shadowy branches snake-free. Settled and as comfortable as she could be given her current location, she said, "I don't have a home."

"Trust me, your mom would like nothing better than for you and your baby to live with her." Using a sparking device, Nash lit the small fire. On his knees, he blew on the struggling flame. "I shouldn't be doing this, but you're going to need protein for our morning hike."

"I'm not eating that snake."

"And you call me stubborn?" He made quick work of raising a stick rack on which to rest their meal.

"Who are you, MacGyver?" Was there anything the man couldn't do?

"Close." He dragged a log closer to the fire, then had a seat. "I'm a SEAL—at least, I used to be."

"Like the ones in movies?"

He shrugged. "I guess."

"How can you be so blasé? That's a big deal. Your mom must be proud."

Stoking the fire, he said, "Point of fact, she hated it. Now, I'm more like a bodyguard and she's all the time asking when I plan to retire or take a safe job selling cars."

For whatever reason, the fact that Nash's mom wasn't proud of her son's achievements made Maisey sad. For as long as she'd known him, he'd wanted to be in the Navy—like his dad. "I assume your mom's feelings have more to do with her already having spent a lifetime worrying about your father?"

"You remember?" Their gazes met and in the fire's glow, she saw him for the man he'd become.

I remember everything. "I was sorry to hear he'd passed."

Most especially, she remembered how much it hurt letting Nash go. Growing up in a broken home had been at times a nightmare. There had been constant bickering and her mother's tears. Nash's house had been her haven. His dad served in the Navy, too. He'd never cheated, but was deployed a huge chunk of his time. When Nash announced he'd enlisted, then proposed, Maisey's gut reaction had been that she wanted no part of being a military wife.

Like your drug lord was so much better?

For the first time since Nash had blown back into her life like a category five storm, she appraised him. He was classically handsome. Square-jawed with a nose crooked from when he'd been hit with a baseball the summer between their junior and senior year. When he was mad, his gray eyes sometimes took on the color of clouds on a stormy day. He used to wear his dark hair on the long side, but he now sported a messy military buzz. After all these years apart, he still took her breath away.

"Mais?" She barely heard him over the fire's crackle and a tree frog determined to steal the show. "What are you thinking?"

"About the night my mom found out about Dad's first affair. I was so upset, that you came over to sleep on our sofa. Mom made us Rice Krispies Treats and we watched the *Wizard of Oz*. We were in fifth grade and quizzed each other on spelling words during commercials."

His laugh flip-flopped her tummy in a way she hadn't felt since she'd first met Vicente. "*Mmm* . . . Your mom truly has a way with Rice Krispies Treats. She made me a batch while we talked about bringing you home."

"She always liked you."

"Feeling's mutual." He rotated his snake and despite her misgivings, she had to admit the delicious scent had her mouth watering.

"How strange is it that here we are, all these years later, about to share a cottonmouth meal in the middle of a swamp?"

"You're going to eat?" His half-smile filled her with the oddest sense that maybe, just maybe, they would be okay.

Then she heard gunshots.

5

"I know there's a gator eyeing us for a snack."

"No chance. You're too salty."

"Ha ha."

It had been hours since they'd heard shots. Dawn streaked the sky with slashes of orange and purple, yet Nash wasn't taking chances. To hide their heat signatures in the event Vicente's men had thermal scopes, Nash doused the fire and took Maisey into the black water alongside their camp. Her teeth hadn't stopped chattering since. He wouldn't tell her, but though he wasn't too concerned about biting creatures sharing their patch of watery real estate, what spooked him was the prospect of Maisey's core temp getting too low. A while back he'd read about four Army Ranger candidates dying during training in a Florida panhandle swamp. The water then had been in the low fifties. Lucky for Maisey and him, August water temps in the Everglades pushed ninety, meaning they shouldn't be in immediate danger from the elements.

She squashed a whiny mosquito on her cheek. "Is this the worst jam you've ever been in?"

"Not even close." Striving for a casual tone, he said, "One time, my team and I were dropped off by Bandar Beyla along the Indian Ocean coast. High winds killed our jump plan. We ended up twenty miles out to sea in a storm so bad I could hardly see my hand in front of my face. Oh—and let's not forget the live nuke we were chasing."

"What happened?" she asked with rapt interest.

"Fifteen hours later, we made shore and completed our mission."

"Which w-was?"

He winked. "If I told you, I'd have to kill you. Ready to get out of here?"

"Think it's s-safe?"

"Come on . . ." *I'll make it safe.* He took her hand, leading her back to their previous camp. Again came the sensation that for once in a very long time he was needed. "But try sloshing as little as possible on the way out."

"O-okay . . ."

With her seated at the base of her cypress, Nash made quick work of restarting the fire. Maisey was soaked and no doubt dehydrated. After cleaning a tin can he'd found along their trek, he rigged it to set over the fire to use for boiling water. The CamelBak vest he wore that had held more than enough water to last for days had been shot. Another fact he preferred to keep to himself.

Her shivering slowed and she held her hands in front of the crackling fire. "A while back, your mom told me you were married and your wife was pregnant. She also told me you . . . lost them."

Not sure what to say—preferring not to discuss his family at all, Nash turned the snake he'd set aside when they'd been interrupted.

"I'm sorry."

"Me, too." More than she'd ever know.

"I always like to think there's a reason for everything, but with your family, and now Vicente, it's hard."

Tensed, he said, "With all due respect, there is no fathomable reason I can see for my beautiful wife and baby to have been taken. For you to suggest there was . . ." A muscle ticked in his jaw. He squeezed his hands into fists, trying to work through the grief her probing raised.

Give him gunfire. Snakes. Bombs. None of it came close to making bile rise in his throat the way talk of his past did.

"Sorry, Nash." He'd crouched in front of the fire and when she placed her hand on his bare forearm, he jolted as if her touch had stung. "Really. In time, you'll—"

"Enough, okay?" The snake meat had turned white, signifying it was fully cooked. He took a third for himself, handing the rest on the spit to her. "Eat. Once you get past what it is, you'll find the taste good."

"You take more."

"Maisey . . ." Never again would he accept a mission involving a female.

"All right. Thanks."

He nodded.

Once she'd finished her portion, he made her drink. Satisfied she and her baby were as adequately nourished as he could manage, he said, "Get some sleep. I'll keep watch."

She opened her mouth—to argue? As if guessing bickering about the request would get her nowhere, she turned to her side, settling in for a rest.

"Here . . ." He gave her a folded rain poncho. Lots of times in less than ideal places, he'd used it as a pillow. Kneeling, he placed it between her head and the tree's rough outer surface. The feel of her soft curls beneath his rough fingertips knotted his throat. Stupid, but how long had it been since he'd performed such a seemingly insignificant act as touching a woman's hair?

Backing away from his charge, he took his seat on the log in front of the fire, glad for the distance between them. For safety from Vicente and his men, as soon as she drifted off, he'd douse the flames. But for now, for morale, she needed them.

"Thank you for this," she said of the makeshift cushion.

"Sure." He liked to think he'd have done the same for anyone, but how many nights had he spent in the field with his teammates and never felt the need to share? "Rest. We'll head out in a few hours—oh, and use this." From another pocket, he withdrew a rolled mosquito net, floating it over her head.

"You really do think of everything."

"Kind of my job."

"Still, thanks." She reached up to take his hand, giving him a light squeeze. "No one's ever done anything like this for me—putting your life on the line to . . ." Tears welled in her eyes. ". . . How did I let things get to this point?"

"I'm guessing you went into the relationship with your heart wide open. Granted, there may have been warning signs, but who's looking for those when everything's going good?"

"True." A sad laugh escaped her. "Once I'm back home, my plan is to steer clear of all men . . ." She patted her belly. "Except for this little guy."

"Sounds reasonable." An image of his wife, Hope, prepping the nursery for their newborn son hit from nowhere. She'd been a space buff and ordered a shuttle mobile to hang over the crib. He hadn't been able to find the right screwdriver to assemble it, and scoured the house in his search. Turned out she'd had it in her back pocket the whole time. He'd razzed her about it for weeks. Now, the pain of losing her was so great, he had to look away. He could literally stand anything other than feeling. Remembering all he'd once had and lost.

Ten minutes later, Maisey drifted off.

Accustomed to going long spells without sleep, Nash wasn't especially tired. He'd planned on dousing the fire. Instead, he repaired the hole in his CamelBak, then set about boiling enough water to see them through the next day.

Humidity and a gunshot had his GPS wonky. Not a major worry as he'd been well trained in old-school compass reading. To prep this mission, he'd plotted escape routes using satellite photos. In a perfect world, calculating a travel time of thirty minutes a mile, come morning they'd make it well before nightfall to the secondary jon boat he'd brought and concealed. From there, it was a four-hour ride to where he'd parked his truck.

Finished with chores, he had two hours till dawn.

Maisey lightly snored.

The heat was still oppressive, but bearable.

Spying a patch of saw palmettos, he filled his free time keeping busy. He wove Maisey a frond mat that might make her rest stops more comfortable and bug free. He also made her a fan with a smooth cypress handle. Crude sandals to reinforce her slippers. It had been a screw-up, not packing her a change of clothes and shoes—just like not anticipating that she wouldn't want to be rescued. He hadn't seen that coming.

He should have anticipated that potential. Like the fire that had taken his wife and unborn child, though he'd been told the faulty wiring in their fixer-upper sparking a flame had been a fluke, it had been preventable. If only he'd had an electrician replace every inch of wiring. If only he'd insured nothing flammable had been anywhere near the master bedroom or that Hope had worn flame retardant PJs to bed instead of one of his T-shirts.

He dropped the palm fronds to press his fingers to his throbbing forehead.

Having reached the expert level on the *If Only* game, he knew the drill. A killer headache typically set in, followed by hours of nausea-inducing guilt. He'd down a half-dozen beers, sleep it off, then wake to a new day.

Here, with Maisey's safety his responsibility, he didn't have the luxury of nursing his pain. He needed to snap out of it and get his head back in the game. But that was kind of hard, considering Maisey's baby bump constantly reminded him of all he'd lost.

Was he jealous that her son was still alive? Hell, yeah. But he was also that much more determined to keep him that way. He'd already lost one woman and child he had promised to protect, and it would never happen again.

As for the personal history between Maisey and him? Old news never to be revisited.

Nash forced himself to focus on his projects.

The insect chatter had a rise and fall rhythm to which he matched his inhalations. Slow breathing helped get his runaway emotions in check. Hope and their unborn son were in a better place, being looked after by a power far more capable than him. As for Maisey, she'd soon be back with her mother— although not in their hometown of Jacksonville as she'd planned. Until Vicente was dead or locked behind bars, Nash feared Maisey and her son might never be truly safe.

But then realistically, could anyone ever be one hundred percent safe?

Lord knew, he'd been a fool for thinking they could.

6

"I've got to rest." Maisey hated being physically weak, but two hours into their trek to the backup boat Nash had hidden, every inch of her body ached. Muscles she hadn't even known existed screamed for relief—even better, a soak in a nice, hot bath.

"You've got five minutes," Nash said. He presented her with the plastic tube from which she'd seen him drinking. Silly, but sharing the mouthpiece struck her as overly intimate.

The last time her lips touched his had been in high school.

She drank, but in the process, inadvertently locked her gaze with his. To her over-sensitized nerves, the sensation was akin to a kiss. Sharply looking away, she drank her fill, then returned the tube.

With her cheeks flushed from the brush of his fingers against hers, it seemed like the perfect opportunity to use the fan Nash had made her.

"Eat this." From the fathomless pits of his cargo pants pockets, he took a protein bar. While it was misshapen and partially melted, never had food tasted so good.

"What about you?"

Kneeling alongside a decaying log with his back to her, he fished for an insect that his pose kept her from seeing. Popping it in his mouth, he chewed.

Fighting not to retch, Maisey asked, "How can you do that?"

"It's called survival. Don't knock it. If we're out here much longer, you might also be dining on grubs."

"Never," she assured with a shudder, fanning all the harder.

"Watch what you say, or you'll jinx us." His smile lit his eyes—gray and crinkled at the corners from time in the sun. She couldn't imagine the kinds of things he'd seen. Didn't want to. But because of him, she was alive. Uncomfortable, but safe. She owed him everything.

Extending her his hand, he helped her back to her feet—no easy task this far into her pregnancy. As if protesting her sudden motion, her baby jolted.

She grimaced.

"What's wrong? You okay?"

Nodding, she said, "This little guy has a way of kicking my ribs that seriously hurts. Wanna feel? He's really on the move."

He reached out, but then drew back. "I'm good. Thanks for the offer, though."

"When your wife was pregnant, did you ever watch her belly?" Realizing that regardless of Nash's answer, the question could be construed as cruel, she covered awkward silence with more of her own chatter. "A few months ago, before learning the kind of man I'd married—correction, *thought* I'd married—Vicente used to be fascinated with studying our son. Sometimes our baby's tiny foot would arc all the way across my belly and Vicente would stare as if he'd never seen a better show. I don't get it. How a man can be two people at once. To me—at least before I'd told him I was leaving—he'd been kind and gentle and caring. Upon realizing I'd not only witnessed him killing his associate but intended to tell police, he transformed to a monster. Sounds corny, but when we married, I'd never felt more vibrant and alive. Now, I feel like the ghost of someone I used to know."

"Ready?" Nash tapped his watch.

"Seriously?" Maisey wasn't sure what she'd expected from Nash after she'd poured out the most intimate details of the life she'd once shared with a madman, but acting as if she'd merely commented on the weather wasn't it. "That's all you have to say?"

Using his machete, he slashed a path for her to follow through thick vegetation. "Sorry for what Vicente put you through, but I asked you last night to stay out of my personal business. Asking me about my dead wife's baby bump?" He slashed harder at the vines blocking their course. "Not cool."

"For what it's worth," she struggled to keep up with his powerful pace, "the second the question left my mouth, I regretted it. Please don't be angry. I—"

"I'm not angry." He stopped alongside a water oak. Arched his neck. He wore a heavy helmet with night vision goggles on top. Sweat dampened his tan complexion and she could only imagine how hot he was under his equipment. Regret weighed heavy on her conscience for making what was already a bad time, worse. "What burns me is how you, my mom, my so-called friends—even your mom—all feel entitled to talk about a private, painful part of my life I'd rather lock in a vault."

"You don't mean that."

"That's another thing—" his renewed slashing took on a desperate feel "—I'm sick of folks telling me what I mean. How I should feel. Get it through your head, what happened to Hope and our unborn son is something I can't even begin to process—don't want to. They meant everything to me, and . .

." He froze.

"What?" she whispered, fearing another snake.

"Listen . . ."

From an impossible to judge distance came un-mistakable baying. Dogs. "Think they're out here for us?"

"Can't say for sure, but if I were a bad guy, tracking my pregnant woman through an impassable swamp, seems like a reasonable way to go."

7

Just when Nash thought his day couldn't get worse....

With hounds baying from what couldn't be more than a mile away, he surveyed the bullet-riddled aluminum jon boat. Stomach fisted, he eyed Maisey who barely had strength to stand. With Vicente having ruined their last best hope of a quick escape, this supposedly simple in-and-out mission had become infinitely more complex.

"Y-you have another backup plan, right?" Her complexion had turned unnaturally pale.

"Sure." Of course, he had a plan, he just hadn't voiced it yet—or, even thought of it. But for sure it was germinating. He hoped.

Removing his helmet, he used his forearm to

wipe sweat from his brow. The day's heat and humidity were brutal. Had he known they'd face this dilemma, he'd have taken the day to rest, opting to travel by night.

"Mind sharing?"

He glanced her way. "What?"

"The plan? Those dogs sound awfully close."

True. "Sorry, but to mask our scent, we're gonna have to hit the water."

Nose wrinkled, she asked, "The black, mossy, foul-smelling water we've counted six hungry gators eyeballing us from?"

"One and the same."

The dog's barks grew more frantic.

Nash took the camo netting from the useless boat, then stood alongside Maisey, wrapping it around them both. "Let's go."

Spying a clump of alligator weed, he broke two lengths of the hollow stems.

Handing one to Maisey, Nash said, "If I give you the signal, as quietly as possible, duck underwater. Use this as a snorkel."

She folded her arms and scowled. "I can't put my head under water. You know that. Remember Allysa Franklin's thirteenth birthday? She had a pool party and Johnny Preston dunked me? I almost drowned."

"Stop the histrionics. And for the record, I saved you." Judging by the frantic baying, the hounds couldn't have been more than a quarter mile away. Nash considered himself unflappable, but his usual companions were SEALs. Without question, they did what needed to be done. Maisey was a delicate unknown. He not only had her to worry about, but her baby. The closer the dogs came, the more he feared he might not be up for this challenge. Palms sweating, pulse racing, he shook off his nerves. This was no time to fold. "When I say, you *will* put that stem in your mouth and duck. Not only your life, but your baby's depends on you following my instructions to the letter. Understand?"

Her doe-eyed stare left him regretting his rough demeanor.

Hand on the small of her back, he led her slowly into the water. When he'd initially covered the boat, he'd laced the camo netting with reeds and grasses. Honestly, he was surprised Vicente hadn't assigned hired guns to wait for them at each boat. It would have been a logical move. The fact that he hadn't made Nash wonder just how adept his team was at hunting human targets. "This waterway looks like it has a slight current. We're going to ride it with this mini-island over our heads. You'll be able to breathe, but I'm not gonna lie—it won't be pleasant. To Vicente's men, we'll look like debris."

The barking and baying was near enough to raise the hair on the back of Nash's neck.

"The bad guys are close, Maisey. This is basic

snorkeling. Piece of cake."

Though her eyes read pure panic, she again nodded. With her teeth already chattering, Nash placed their odds at about fifty/fifty in making a clean escape. Toss in the gator/snake/hypothermia/wild-card factor and it was shaping up to be a seriously lousy day.

Having reached the center of the narrow channel's flow, Nash adjusted the net in time to spot a hound alternately baying and lapping at the algae-covered water's edge.

Maisey whispered, "He doesn't look like he wants to kill us, does he?"

"All he wants is to find our scent."

Crashing foliage and a deep, Southern drawl alerted Nash that the dog's master wasn't far behind. "Stupid mutt. Told Vicente to search with a heli, but he said it would draw too much attention."

"Ask me," a new voice sounded through tall grasses, "Vicente's pretty little thing is long gone. This search is a waste of time." Approaching a second frantically barking dog, the man patted him between his ears. "What're you all excited about?"

"Got your *snorkel* ready?" Nash whispered in Maisey's ear. The current was painstakingly slow in clearing them from danger.

Fingers trembling, she held it for him to see.

"Good girl. On the count of three, we're both going to slowly descend. Got it?"

"Uh huh . . ."

"One . . ."

"Hey, there, fella. See something?" one of the men called to his dog.

A bald hulk of a man sporting full sleeve tattoos and a goatee, stared right at them. Nash had taken special care weaving plants through the netting and knew to the men onshore they looked like a floating isle of weeds, but that didn't stop the event from being unnerving.

"Two . . ."

Having entered upstream of where their hunters had emerged from dense undergrowth, Nash and Maisey were ten yards from being dead even with them. If his pulse raced much faster, he feared passing out. On his own or with his team, there was no emotion—only adrenaline in its purest form, something that sharpened frayed nerves. Now, he was consumed by *what if* scenarios and concern for Maisey that he couldn't control.

"Popcorn, what the heck are you—"

Before Nash could give Maisey her signal to duck, an eight-foot gator erupted from the shoreline's thick algae, snapping off the nearest hound's right front leg. Before the dog's handler fully grasped what was happening, the gator returned to finish his meal, dragging the howling canine into the water until the swamp fell eerily silent.

"That slimy fucker killed my best hunting

hound!"

"This is voodoo. I'm out of here."

Breathing shallow, Nash could only imagine the riot raging in Maisey's chest. He wanted to comfort her, but couldn't risk the movement. No matter how distracted Vicente's men might currently be, there was no guarantee they might not look up to discover their intended targets right before them.

Maisey silently cried. Lips pressed tight, silvery tears streaked mud on her cheeks. He admired her for holding her emotions in check, but he'd be lying if he said he didn't wish for the right thing to say to calm her.

"I'm gonna kill you, stupid sumbitch!" The dog's owner used an M16 to shoot wildly at the water.

Though mini-explosions formed a wake and turned algae into projectiles, Nash held firm to Maisey. She, in turn, clung to him so tightly he wouldn't be surprised to find bruises. Which was all right. Whatever she needed to get her through.

Over and over the guy fired his weapon, not stopping until running out of ammo.

Ten feet upstream, the gator rose belly-up to the surface.

What remained of the dog followed.

Maisey tensed alongside him. Little convulsions told him she wasn't in a good way.

"Relax," he whispered in her ear. "Everything's

going to be fine.

"No. No, it's not." Though she'd spoken so softly he'd hardly heard her words, the panic in her eyes and complexion's pall said more than she ever could to describe her terror.

"Shh . . ." Temporarily releasing her to bracket her face with his hands, he begged, "Trust me. We're almost home free." For a moment, he lost himself in her achingly familiar blue gaze. They were no longer in a swamp, but on her mom's back porch, on the verge of sharing a kiss. What was wrong with his mind that it had chosen now for a trek down memory lane?

"Nash?" She licked her lips. Her pupils widened, and if possible, her eyes grew even wider.

"Yeah?" He didn't even know the asshole inside him who couldn't look away from her plump mouth.

"In case we don't make it, thank you for trying."

"Stop. We'll be fine." *Assuming I forget the way things used to be between us long enough to focus on the task at hand.*

Then, the unthinkable happened when the dog's owner crashed into the water. The dog's body had floated into the current and was now a mere five feet from Nash and Maisey.

"Leave him!" The guy still on shore urged.

"No! He was a good dog and deserves a decent burial." Who knew? A thug with heart.

Nash's adrenaline spiked. "I need both hands.

Think you can hold on to me?"

Maisey's answer was to hug his chest.

"Good girl . . ."

Hands free, with their hunter fifteen feet away and the dog practically on top of them, Nash withdrew his Glock that he'd already outfitted with a sound suppressor. Given luck, the goon would be too focused on his dog to inspect floating grass.

"Stupid waste of life," Vicente's man mumbled on his approach to his dog.

Nash pushed past his latest swell of nerves.

"He was a good boy."

The dog was now three feet from Nash.

Maisey tucked herself behind him.

His pulse thundered in his ears.

The guy was now in water over his head. His thrashing strokes surged the dog's body against the grass-covered mat. Unless the man was fully focused on his pet, there was no possible way he and Maisey wouldn't be discovered.

"Sorry, boy. You shouldn't have—"

In his struggle to tread water, the guy kicked Nash. Time froze for the instant it took him to realize he wasn't alone. He tossed the netting aside, shouting to his friend on shore, "Hey! Found them!"

Bullets ripped the water.

With no way to escape, Nash did what he'd been trained to do—double-tap the forehead of the man shooting at them from shore.

Maisey screamed.

The guy in the water grabbed for Nash, but lacked the swimming strength to stay afloat. Nash lunged for him, but the guy had been smart enough to swim underwater for shallower ground. Once able to stand, he sloshed for shore, snatching up his weapon with one hand and radio with the other. Simultaneously, he radioed for back-up and shot wildly at the water.

"Duck!" Nash shouted to Maisey.

The guy had lost it, firing dozens of rounds to the accompaniment of his own roar. When he was forced to stop shooting long enough to reload, Nash made his second kill of the day.

Maisey had floated further downstream and now cried hysterically. "You killed him!"

"What else was I supposed to do?" Nash shouted back. "It was us or them, and sorry, but I'm not in the mood to die."

Having reached her, he tried lightly grasping her in a lifeguard-style hold, but she wasn't having it. "Let me go! I can't take this anymore!"

Ignoring her protests in favor of getting her safely ashore, Nash grabbed the back of her shirt, dragging her as best he could.

From over the dead guy's radio, a tinny voice asked, "LeFlour, copy? You there?" Was that Vicente on the other end? "Did I hear right and you caught the intended targets? LeFlour? Come in! What's your location?"

Once Nash delivered Maisey to the muddy shore, he started to gut the radio, but then thought better. Information could be gleaned from chatter.

Nash put his hand over his mouth to muffle his voice. "False alarm. I repeat false alarm."

"We heard shots."

"Wildlife kill. No sign of your lady, sir."

"Keep looking!"

"You're no better than Vicente." Maisey sat up, hugging her massive belly. Rocking and crying with her hands over her face. "You shot those men right between their eyes."

"Woman, are you crazy?" Searching the dead for usable equipment, Nash could scarcely contain his rage. "I killed those two men for our safety—your baby's. They shot at us first. Dozens of rounds. It's a miracle we're even alive."

She was back to shivering. Teeth chattering, she continued sobbing.

"You and me?" Kneeling before her, he tucked his fingertips beneath her chin, forcing her to meet his gaze. "We're in a war. People *are* going to die. The goal is for those people to not be us."

She nodded.

"No," he again forced her gaze to his. "Look me in the eyes and tell me you understand I'm not a stone-cold killer like your ex."

"I do, but this is all too much."

"Agreed." He took a bandana from a pocket, then cleaned it with drinking water. "Things got dicey there for a sec, but all's good now."

"*Good?*" Her sad laugh rode the fringe of madness. "Oh—our situation is far from good. I'm cold and hungry and tired and thirsty and that dead man won't stop staring at me." Hand trembling, she pointed at the nearest corpse. "Plus, Vicente said over the radio he heard gunfire. That means he's not far behind."

As tenderly as he could, Nash wiped tear-streaked mud from Maisey's cheeks. He stroked it from her forehead and nose and chin. When she closed her eyes and exhaled, he cleaned her brows and the smile lines at the corners of her eyes. And when she opened those eyes, he leaned forward, resting his forehead against hers. "I *will* protect you."

"I know." For the first time that day, her voice rang strong. Sincere. Her trust further heightened his resolve to see her and her baby safely through.

She exhaled. Her warm breath hit his lips, tightening his stomach in a way he hadn't felt in well over the year his wife had been gone. While the sensation was far from unpleasant, it was also unwelcome. Retreating to a safe distance, he asked, "Hungry?"

"Very. What's on the menu? Snake? Gator?"

"Actually . . ." Nash eyed the still-fresh gator kill lying on the shore. "Seems a shame for the little guy to have died in vain."

"Little guy?" She laughed. "That alligator is longer than I am."

8

An hour later, while Maisey sat in relative comfort on a log, using her new palm frond fan, she watched with awe as Nash performed yet another crafty task. Using vines and sticks and a vicious knife, he'd constructed a rack on which he'd hung chunks of meat. He'd stripped the alligator and butchered it and already had a nice, juicy section roasting over a fire.

While he'd buried the bad guys in shallow graves, her job was to listen and observe. The slightest change in bird calls or a cracked twig. Gunfire. Baying dogs. Anything outside of their current norm.

"Nash?" She slowed her fanning.

"Yes, ma'am?" Like back when they'd been in

high school, his stoic expression was entirely too mesmerizing. Too brimming with the kind of innate self-assurance that was earned. If possible, he seemed more at ease here in the middle of a swamp than he ever had back in Jacksonville. He wasn't just in his element, but seemed to have invented it.

"What do you think happened to the other hound? Is he okay?"

He paused in his digging with a collapsible shovel to frown. "My fear is that he ran straight home to his food dish and comfy bed. Don't get me wrong, I love dogs as much as the next guy, but when he returned without his doggy friend or two handlers, it's not that great a leap for whoever's on the other end to realize there was trouble."

"Oh." She hadn't thought of it that way.

"That's why I need you to stay alert. We shouldn't have this fire, but this much protein is hard to come by and you and the baby need regular meals."

"What's gator taste like?"

"Chewy chicken. Better than cottonmouth—though some of my team might find that debatable."

"Tell me about them."

"Who?" Head cocked, he used his sleeve to wipe sweat from his forehead.

"The team you mentioned."

He covered the last of the two graves with vines. "The guys on my SEAL team—or, I guess that would be ex-team?"

She nodded.

"We still run missions, so sometimes it gets screwed up in my head. Anyway, me and Jasper, Harding, Everett and a bunch of other guys went through BUD/S together which—not gonna lie—was pretty intense."

Forehead furrowed, she said, "For those of us who aren't ninja warriors, what's that?"

"Basic Underwater Demolition/SEAL training. It was months of straight-up torture. Swimming in open sea until I literally thought my limbs were frozen. Finally getting to dry land only to run twenty-miles carrying a raft on our heads, followed by another swim and push-ups. No way could I have gotten through it without the help of my friends. We might now be out of the Navy, but we're still tight, protecting everyone from presidents to pregnant chicks like you." His grin and wink combo were swoon-worthy.

Why had she left him?

Mrs. Adamson had been a lucky woman.

Head bowed, she asked softly, "How did you meet your wife?"

His grin faded. "Remember when I asked you not to talk about my family? I meant it."

"Sorry . . ." Her heart ached for him. "But it's not natural for you to act as if your wife and baby never even existed. Wouldn't you rather celebrate the good they brought to your life than dwell on the bad?"

"Correct me if I'm wrong," he snapped while adding more wood to the fire, "but isn't there a proverb about folks living in glass houses not throwing stones? If I think about how good Hope and I had it, I'll lose my shit. I don't hear you waxing poetic about how our pal Vicente wooed you with roses and diamonds. At the moment, pretty much all you can wrap your head around is the fact that you not only married a psycho, but weren't even legit married. But wait—like that's not bad enough, he's doing everything in his power to ensure you only live long enough to give birth to his son. Do I have it right?"

His words stung to her core—not only because they hurt, but because he was right. She had no moral business trying to counsel him when her own life needed plenty of work. Throat tight, she willed tears to stay at bay, but they went ahead and fell. She longed to rail at Nash, demanding an answer to how he could be so cruel, but deep inside, she knew her own truth. The terror she felt over bringing her innocent baby into such a tumultuous world. Would she even be a fit mom? How could she when she hadn't even been smart enough to realize the guy she'd fallen for was an already-married killer?

"Sorry." Nash stood before her, hands in his back pockets.

"It's okay." Maisey lacked the strength to meet

his gaze. "I had it coming. I promised I wouldn't talk about your wife, but I did it anyway." After a sharp exhale and brush of tears from her cheeks, she said, "I won't make that mistake again."

They shared the surprisingly tasty meal in silence.

Maisey ate until she felt near popping, then for her baby, forced herself to eat a little more. She drank deeply of the water Nash had so carefully boiled. She'd done all of that without either of them saying a word.

After swatting a whiny mosquito, she asked, "Ever talking to me again?"

He half-heartedly glanced her way before taking a bite from his latest chunk of meat.

"Goody!" She clapped her hands with forced glee. "I love the silent game. Even back in third grade, you always were the master."

"Knock it off," he finally said.

"So you are capable of speech?"

He shook his head. "I'm capable of a lot of things. Don't test me."

Maisey rolled her eyes. "I've survived attack dogs, gators and gun-toting bad guys. You, Nash Adamson, don't scare me one iota. In fact, I think behind your tough guy routine, you're a big soft—"

Before she finished her sentence, Nash pitched his meal to the ground. He clamped his hand over her mouth, whispering into her ear, "Not another word."

9

The whole time maisey yammered about feelings, Nash sensed they were being watched.

It wasn't until he detected a metallic glint in the sun that he forcibly shut Maisey the hell up. Had she forgotten where they were? Who wanted them dead? At this point, he wouldn't put it past Vicente to carve out his son and leave Maisey's remains for the gators. She needed to get a clue and realize how grave their situation actually was.

She breathed hard against him. Her every forced inhalation burned his lungs. As much as he hated the fact, he couldn't deny the two of them still shared a soul-deep connection. He'd assumed with the passage of time, the thread binding them would have frayed, but it had held surprisingly strong, making him all the more confused about what he felt for her when he should have remained focused on the task at hand.

He'd screwed the pooch by tipping his hat to the fact that he knew Vicente's men were out there. He should have let her rattle on while silently waiting for his chance to pop off whoever lurked in the shadows. He hadn't been prepared for how much her poking at old wounds would throw him off balance. He never should have charged to her rescue—not when he was already screwed in the head. If he hadn't been pissed about her bringing up his wife again, he would have noticed sooner that they had company.

"Real slow," he whispered, working overtime to ignore how familiar and right her soft curves felt against his hard angles, "we're going to move around to the other side of this cypress. Nod if you understand."

She did.

The seconds it took to get her to the marginally safe place lasted an eternity.

He tried not to be rough about pushing her into the buttress formed by the ancient tree's roots. Assuming Vicente's men weren't smart enough to attack from above, she'd be safe on three sides.

"Take this." He handed her his best knife. "Whatever you hear, don't move unless you're directly threatened. Understand?"

Wide-eyed with silent tears forging streams down her dirty cheeks, she nodded.

Nash hated leaving her, but had no choice.

The stench of cigarette smoke rose above the musky swamp.

A cough reached through the impenetrable vines and grasses, making the sound seem to come from everywhere all at once. Judging by where Nash had seen the glint of sun on metal, the bastard couldn't have been out more than twenty yards. The bigger question—was he alone?

After one last glance at Maisey, he raised his dry and ready-for-action Glock, then crept east of their temporary camp. With sun streaming through low-hanging Spanish moss, birds chirping and a woodpecker going to town on the rotting carcass of a dead cypress, the scene might have been idyllic were it not for the cottonmouth slithering into black water five feet off to his right.

Needing to draw out their latest enemy, Nash knelt to grab a rock, then pitched it up and over his current locale as far as possible, given the dense foliage. The plan worked. The dufus fired a few rounds in the wrong direction.

Now that Nash had his location, he doubled back, placing himself behind the guy for a swift, silent slit of his throat.

Nash helped himself to his M16 and supply pack that was near bulging with bug spray, bottled water, granola bars, beef jerky and Cheetos. Score. Wasn't exactly nutritious, but it beat the hell out of grubs.

"Buck?" a voice called from the green gloom. "You okay?"

Shit. Buck had company.

Buck's friend fired a few rounds. "Damned snakes."

For now, Nash abandoned the dead man's gear in favor of neutralizing his companion.

Luckily, he was about as graceful as a wild hog and just as easy to pick off. As soon as Nash had a clean shot, he nailed him between his eyes.

His gear was even better. Nice big knife and way better chow—a few Mountain House freeze-dried meals and even a jet boil with all sorts of nifty accessories. Nash took it all. The guy even had a hammock and working GPS. Relief shimmered through him. With the supplies he'd gained, he could stay out here months, but Maisey couldn't. The sooner he returned her to civilization, the better.

After dragging both corpses to watery graves, Nash erased all trackable signs of anyone's presence, then slung both men's packs and weapons over his shoulders for the short return trek to Maisey.

A hot meal could do wonders for morale, so he planned to get her nice and full on gator steak and sweet and sour chicken, then settled into the hammock for a good night's sleep. In the morning, the

GPS would get them to a road that would lead to a cheeseburger and a nice, soft bed—not necessarily in that order.

Nash couldn't wait to safely deliver Maisey to her mother. The poor woman had been out of her mind with worry. He remembered Maisey as a feisty, determined girl who never failed to speak her mind or gladly accept any dare—no matter how outrageous. Case in point—when he'd stupidly dared her on a class zoo field trip to jump into a turtle pond, and she'd dragged him along with her. They'd spent a month in detention, but at least they'd been together. What had that bastard Vicente done to reduce her to this shadow of her former self?

What would it take to bring back the sparkle to her blue eyes?

Nash struggled with the notion that he wanted to be the one who not only saved her from her fake hubby, but from herself as well. He wanted to erase the self-doubt that had settled into her soul, making her believe she was anything less than the perfect girl he'd always known her to be.

Picking his way over rotting logs and tangled vines, it occurred to Nash that for the first time since losing Hope and their baby, he felt not only alive, but filled with purpose. Funny how he'd set out to save Maisey, but in a sense, she was unwittingly returning the favor.

In the time since Nash's former teammate and

friend, Harding, had temporarily booted him from the private security firm they'd founded, Nash had put a new roof on his mom's house, and helped a half-dozen of her widowed or single neighbors with odds-and-end home repairs and in general pissed around feeling sorry for himself. But all that had to end.

As soon as Vicente was either safely behind bars or eliminated, everything would change. Nash would make a run to Denver, where their team had set up shop. Tell Harding he was ready to be put back on the assignment list. Just because Hope was gone, didn't mean there weren't plenty of other folks needing help. If anything, in her memory, Nash figured he should work harder to assist others in need.

Everyone in need? Or only petite blonds you once had a thing for?

He ignored the snarky voice in his head to forge through more tangled vines.

Any of the guys in Trident, Inc. would feel the same. Man, woman or child—if someone needed protection, they'd each be willing to fight. As for the fact that Nash's first mission outside of Trident happened to be ensuring the safety of an old friend, that was nothing more than a coincidence. The fact that Maisey hadn't only unwittingly awoken the long-slumbering warrior in him, but something else…

He refused to go there.

She was pregnant and in danger. Nash was her

protector—nothing more.

He quickened his pace to return to her, fighting forbidden flashes of time they'd shared. Okay, so yeah, a million years ago, he'd planned his entire life around her. They'd talked marriage and babies. But then she'd dumped him, because she'd never wanted to be a military spouse. Her dad met her mom while he'd been stationed at Mayport, near Jacksonville, Florida. Nash's dad had been stationed there, too. The difference was that his father had been a loyal, loving husband up until three years ago when he'd passed of a heart attack. Maisey's dad was still alive and well and—Nash assumed—sleeping with a different woman every night. Maisey had been an accident, and he'd married her mom, but only stayed around long enough for her to get out of diapers. When Nash and Maisey had been kids, he remembered her dad showing up for birthdays and Christmases, but that was about it. Her mother never divorced him, and as far as Nash knew, had never been with another man. The whole thing was tragic, which made the mess that had become of Maisey's life that much tougher to bear.

Maybe Nash could help her adjust to her new routine? Clearly, they'd never again be lovers, but at least friends.

He used a machete to hack his way out of a particularly nasty mangrove patch, then five minutes later exited from the foliage to reach their temporary camp.

"Mais?" Nash rounded the tree he'd instructed her to stay beside, only to have his heart catch in his throat.

This couldn't be.

Was he in the wrong place?

He swung around to check for landmarks. The fire still burned. The gator still hung on the spit. His CamelBak hung from a low branch, but the spot where he'd told Maisey to stay put was now empty.

Where the hell had she gone?

Pulse hammering, Nash struggled to find her trail, then he made a sick discovery. He picked up her trail easy enough, then followed it to a place where the muddied ground and flattened brush showed evidence of a struggle. Nash's heart fell as he made out four sets of tracks moving away—clearly not Maisey's. She wasn't walking, because she was being carried by Vicente or one of his men.

10

A twig snapped.

Not long after Nash left, the sound jolted Maisey from a deep sleep.

Her gaze darted about their latest encampment, but when she saw nothing out of sorts, she drifted off again.

Beneath closed eyes, sunlight played through the branches high above her head, forming a lacy pattern that made it easy to believe she was back home with all of this behind her. Shots hadn't been fired, and she was no longer in a swamp, but in the park.

Dreaming of a picnic.

Of lying on a blanket spread over tall, swaying grass. Her baby boy rested beside her, giggling while she tickled his tiny nose with a dandelion. Nash was there, too. Not sharing her blanket, but standing watch. He carried a menacing gun and wore all black—cargo pants, T-shirt, boots, and gear. He hadn't said a word. Just stared at her in that intense way he had back when they'd still been in high school, and she'd told him she'd never marry him

His eyes were dark, expression unreadable.

Her heart ached from the loss of not only her lover, but her best friend.

Maisey woke again.

The dream left her with an uneasy yearning for the way things used to be. She and Nash had finished each other's sentences and laughed over jokes no one found funny but them. She'd never quite understood how things had gone so wrong, so fast . . .

On a blistering May afternoon at their neighborhood pool—a week from graduation—Maisey and Nash shared a cherry snow cone on lounge chairs crammed together near the diving board. He leaned forward, licking syrup from her chin. "Marry me."

"What?" She couldn't help but laugh. Not only was his question silly, but his tongue tickled.

"You heard me."

"I thought you were joking?"

"I'm not."

"What about college?"

He frowned. "I can't go. Mom said we don't have the money. I signed up for the Navy and leave for basic a couple weeks after graduation." He looked down, probably because

he knew if he met her gaze, he'd find fury.

She'd balled her hands into tight fists. How many times had she told him how she felt about the military? Soldiers were brave and strong and a wonderful necessity for the country, but in her experience, they weren't so good at being part of families. Case in point—her own father. He'd hurt Maisey's mother so many times over the years that she'd lost count. Granted, not every man cheated on his spouse, but deployment tossed open the door for marital discord to march in. Why her mother never divorced him was a mystery. She claimed it was because she was a God-fearing woman, and wanted to honor her lifelong vow. But Maisey believed she'd secretly always hoped he'd change.

"Say something," Nash had coaxed.

"You ruined everything. What's wrong with you?" Hot tears flooded her cheeks, and her throat ached from what she could only label as betrayal. "You know how I feel, and you did it anyway. I hate you." She landed a half-hearted slug against his stupid chest, and tried pushing herself up, but he caught her wrists, tugging her back down

In the tussle, she'd dropped the snowcone. It now melted in a sad red pool on the ground.

"You love me." He said. "Marry me, and we'll make all our dreams come true. You can still go to college, and I'll work hard and be an officer. We'll travel the world on the government's dime. It'll be great. You'll see."

"All I see is an idiot. You know what my father did. Why can't you understand?"

He kissed her. Soft and sweet. And like always, it was

never enough. When it came to Nash, she could have kissed him all day, every day and it would still never be anywhere near enough.

"What I understand," he said, "is that your dad hurt you. I get it. But, baby, that doesn't mean I would ever do the same. Look at how great my dad is. Practically every kid we go to school with is a Navy brat, and tons of them have turned out fine. You can't condemn an entire organization based on the faults of one disgusting pig."

But she had.

After telling Nash she never wanted to see him again, she hadn't—up until he'd shown up to rescue her. His being here for her now made no sense. Not after she'd failed on all fronts to be there for him. When her mom told her his wife and unborn child had died, she could have called—at the very least, sent a note—but she hadn't.

Just like she hadn't reached out before that, when she'd learned he'd become a SEAL or when his dad had passed. Why?

Because she'd given up the right to celebrate his successes or mourn his failures and sorrows when she'd turned her back on him all those years ago.

Obviously, her biggest regret centered on ever having succumbed to Vicente's snake-like charm. But coming in a close second would have to be her naïve refusal to give Nash's way a chance. What if everything had gone as he'd said? And he had been a man of his word? And they'd since made a beautiful family?

Maisey hugged her belly.

How different would her life now be if this child were Nash's instead of Vicente's? The thought crushed her. She was soon going to be a mom. She had to start making better decisions—not merely for her sake, but the baby's. With Vicente out of the picture, she'd get back to her career.

Maisey and her longtime friend, Delia, were part-owners in a used clothing store. It wasn't much, but it had been theirs—at least until Vicente whisked her away. When she'd told him she was pregnant, he'd proposed and then paid off her share of the business as well as her student loans for her fashion merchandising degree. Assuming she'd never need or want for anything ever again, she'd naïvely signed over her share of *Glad Rags*.

How had she been so desperate for love that she'd missed a ridiculous number of signs that Vicente wasn't quite what he'd seemed? Paying for everything in cash, cutting her off from family and friends, always needing to be the one in control. From day one, he'd shown classic signs of being an emotional abuser, yet she'd been so eager to erase the pain of having been abandoned by her father, that she'd swallowed Vicente's lies hook, line, and proverbial sinker.

She set Nash's knife atop a wide cypress knob, then drew a flower with her fingertip in the loamy soil.

If she had willingly, quietly gone with Nash when he'd first appeared, they'd no doubt be home by now. This whole mess was her fault, and she hated that she'd dragged her oldest, dearest friend along for the ride.

Something splashed in the nearby black water.

Maisey looked toward the noise, expecting to find a gator or wild hog or some other biting creature, but there was nothing save for a light breeze rustling leaves on the vines and trees.

"Nash? Is that you?" She found herself craving him. His quiet strength.

She angled, pushing herself up to greet him, but got a nasty surprise when her gaze landed not on Nash's familiar black boots, but instead a pair of muck-crusted, camo-patterned hip waders.

"Not so fast." When Maisey tried standing, a man pushed her back down. Three more men silently surrounded her.

She opened her mouth to scream, but before she could take a breath, the nearest man slapped duct tape over her lips.

The knife. Where had she set it? Her gaze turned frantic.

Where had these guys come from? Where was Nash? Was he all right?

Ignoring her muffled shrieks, the men zip-tied her wrists and ankles, then hefted her onto a stretcher.

"*Letmegoooo!*" She struggled as much as she could, but quickly found too much exertion made it impossible to breathe. "*Heeeellllp!*" Her garbled cries were as ineffective as her physical struggles.

When one of the men got too close, Maisey pinched the back of his hand hard enough to draw blood.

"Bitch!" He backhanded her just before her world faded to black.

11

"*Shit, shit, shit . . .*"

Leaving the fire, leaving his gear save for guns, ammo and knives, Nash shot into action, easily tracking a group of four men who must have carried Maisey.

When their boot prints vanished into black water, he followed creamy swirls of mud. With the trail this fresh, they couldn't have gone far. He never should have left her. This was all his fault.

Nash charged faster and faster through stinking muck, uncaring when vines clawed his forehead, nose and cheeks. His whole life had converged to one goal—getting Maisey back.

The sun would soon set, which would give him an additional edge, assuming Vicente's men failed to follow light discipline.

If only I hadn't started that fire. If only I'd taken her with me.

Sickened by his mistakes, Nash forged deeper into the wild until the scent of wood smoke alerted him that he was nearing the enemy camp. Hugging the shadows, he caked mud over his exposed skin, then crept to the edge of the clearing.

Their camp held all the luxuries of home—canvas chairs, a folding table loaded with assorted gear and ammo, hammocks with mosquito netting. Best of all, a twenty-foot air boat, equipped with twelve 175-watt halo lights that would turn night into day. Since Maisey was nowhere to be seen, Nash guessed she'd already been loaded onto the boat. But if that was the case, why weren't her captors already headed back to Vicente? This kind of equipment didn't come cheap. If he'd shelled out a hundred grand for a boat, Nash would expect him to demand results.

Something about this whole scene didn't set right.

While three guys kicked back in their chairs, downing freeze-dried food packs, a fourth pissed. They seemed to be killing time. Why?

A radio squawked, then: "You have my attention."

A mountain of a man rose from the chair nearest the table. He wore hip waders and traditional green camo. He smiled while palming the radio he'd taken from his belt—also green.

Nash, assuming he'd be in and out of Vicente's compound under cover of darkness, had opted for all-black. As had Vicente's men . . .

He narrowed his gaze. If this crew wasn't part of Vicente's team, then who the hell were they?

"Good to hear. So listen," Mountain Man said into the mic, "we heard through the grapevine that you're lookin' for a preggers gal."

"Yes . . ."

Mountain Man leered. "We might have her—for a price."

There was a long pause, during which Nash's heart damn near beat out of his chest. To be clear, he was now not only dealing with a crazy drug lord ex and his thugs, but kidnappers? Maisey was a freaking scum magnet.

"I'm listening. Can you prove you have my property?"

"You want a finger or toe?" This raised belly laughs in his pals.

"She is not to be harmed. Let me speak with her."

"No can do, buddy. See—here's the deal. She's wearing a little nightie, and her baby bump is looking real cute. How about you leave me a million large on the south end of Milk Cay's picnic pavilion, then I'll be sure your lady makes it back to you with her baby still in her belly."

"I'll pay—whatever you want. Don't hurt the child."

"Well, alrighty, then. Sounds like we've got us a deal. What time works for you?"

"Now."

"You have that much cash on hand? Because, look, I might be a redneck, but even I know a bank's gonna take a day or two to drum up that kind of dough."

"I'm not using a bank, and let's make it two million. Bring her—*now.*"

A guy with more hair in his ginger beard than on his head busted out in a maniacal giggle. "By God, this is really gonna work. T-Bone, you the man."

"Damn straight I am." Mountain Man, AKA T-Bone, took a bow.

"Do we have an agreement? Where are you? When are we making the exchange?"

"Hold your horses there, partner. If you can get your hands on two million, maybe I might want four."

This drew applause from his greedy onlookers.

"Damn straight, you do!"

"Whatever. I'm tiring of this game. I'll meet you at the appointed location in an hour. Agreed?"

"Hell, yeah. See you soon."

It took every shred of willpower Nash had not

to finish him where he stood, then take his chances with the others.

Nash aimed his sight at T-Bone's forehead, but if he dropped him within view of the others, they'd return his favor. He needed to play this cool. Drop them one at a time, then, while they sorted whether it was gators or ghosts doing the killing, he'd eventually get them all, leaving the boat free for Maisey and him to use as their ticket out of this swamp.

Besides, still not knowing her location, he couldn't chance stray bullets finding her by mistake.

While the boys celebrated their unexpected windfall, Nash crept around the camp perimeter until reaching the boat, his stomach fisted with nerves. Sure enough, Maisey was unconscious on a stretcher. The sight of her lying pale and prone squeezed his chest to the point of pain. A bruise shadowing her right cheek made his trigger finger itchy. The tape over her mouth made him want to use a rocket launcher on these asshats. She was breathing, though, which he took as about the only good sign. Her legs and arms were covered in bug bites, dirt and scratches. Her once adorable blond curls were a tangled mess.

But she was alive.

At the moment, that was all the motivation Nash needed.

Then Ginger Beard caught Nash climbing in the boat. "Hey! What the hell do you think you're doin'?"

Before Nash had raised his weapon, his opponent fired off three poorly-aimed rounds.

12

Maisey played possum with her captors until her nostrils flared, recognizing Nash's earthy smell.

She opened her eyes in time to see him leap over the boat's side, then drop the bearded man who'd fired at him.

She winced when Nash shoved her stretcher toward the boat's bow, where the higher metal sides would protect her.

He fired off a few more blind rounds, sliced her wrist and ankle restraints, then ducked to say, "Hey, beautiful. Fingers crossed, maybe T-Bone left the key to this rig in the ignition. Take the tape off yourself—it'll hurt less. Oh—and here . . ." He thrust a gun into her hand. "Cover me. Safety's off. Point and shoot."

In the time it took him to duck-walk to the back of the craft, Maisey suffered at least five heart attacks. Was this really happening?

Ripping the duct tape off her mouth stung like she'd been burned. Her first gulp of air tasted like ambrosia. Then reality set in.

She rose up and fumbled with the gun. With shot after shot being fired at them, adrenaline kicked in, and she fired her first round, not expecting to hit anyone, but at least hoping to dissuade the three remaining men from approaching.

"Good job!" Nash hollered when she'd squeezed her eyes and managed to shoot two more rounds. In movies, guns aren't as loud—or as hard to hold onto. Her arms ached from the concussive force. "Keep it up!"

"Shoot the bitch!" one of the bad guys shouted.

"Are you crazy?" another one said. "If she's dead, we don't get paid. Aim for the hull! They won't get far!"

Maisey sent up silent thanks when Nash brought the airboat's engine roaring to life. When the men did fire at the boat, assuming she was no longer their primary target, Maisey worked up her courage to shoot again, this time, keeping her eyes open to hopefully have better aim. Elbows locked, she pointed at the guy with the biggest gun and held her breath before squeezing the trigger. Though she lurched when the first round fired, she kept shoot-ing. The noise made her ears ring, and when Nash moved the boat from land to water, her legs turned to rubber beneath her. She collapsed backwards on-to a padded bench seat.

Suddenly, they were no longer pointed toward the bad guys, but across a lovely stretch of water. The beauty of the violet and orange-streaked sky fueled her soul. They'd made it. At least for the moment, they were safe.

The airboat's motor was deafening.

On instinct, Maisey dropped the gun to cover her ears.

When she felt a tap on her right shoulder, she jumped in surprise, only to see Nash reaching to-ward her with a pair of heavy duty, soundproofing headphones. He immediately returned to steering the boat, which left her feeling bereft. The whole time she'd been held captive, the only reason she hadn't died from fright was because deep inside she'd known that as long as he was alive, he'd never let anything happen to her.

The further down the winding waterway they traveled, the more exhaustion took hold. Maisey's shoulders sagged and in the darkening balmy air, the earth released a loamy-scented sigh.

She closed her eyes and dreams replaced reality. Nash again charged to her rescue, but not in a swamp. This time, they were on Parker Elementary

School's playground.

"Get off the swing!" Dillon Hinkle was the fifth-grade bully, and to show Maisey he meant business, he grabbed the swing's chains, shaking them and her.

"No!" Refusing to budge, she raised her chin. She'd waited in line for her turn fair and square. Everyone knew you got twenty times back and forth before you were supposed to let the next person ride.

"Yes!" He jerked the chains hard enough for her to fall off.

"Ouch! You're mean!" She didn't want to cry, but the gravel beneath the swing cut her hands and knees. There was a little blood and her scraped skin stung.

Maisey looked for the teacher, but she was way far away, talking with her teacher friends.

Dillon stuck out his tongue, then climbed on the swing. If Maisey hadn't rolled out of the way, he'd have kicked her.

The other kids in line knew the bell would ring before Dillon got off, so they ran for the slide and monkey bars.

Maisey was going to run, too, but then her friend and neighbor, Nash, showed up. They were in the same grade, but he usually played basketball or soccer at recess with the older kids. Their moms were friends, and he walked Maisey to and from school every day. He was really tall and cute—but she never told him that!

"Give Maisey her turn," he said to Dillon.

"Screw you!" Dillon kept right on swinging.

While Maisey sat on the ground gaping over Dillon's naughty words, Nash grabbed the swing's chains and jerked

Dillon to a stop. "You going to get off?"

"Screw you! You're not the boss of me!"

Nash had a funny smile—not happy. Maybe more scary.

He started pushing Dillon. Higher and higher he pushed until she thought he was going to flip over. She'd heard of kids doing that, but never actually seen it happen. The faster and higher Dillon flew, the louder he screamed until he was crying and begging for Nash to stop.

Nash did.

Once Dillon planted his feet on the ground, Nash whispered something to him and the kid scrammed.

"What'd you say?" Maisey asked Nash.

"Doesn't matter." The smile he gave her was the cute one that made her tummy feel funny. "Wanna swing?"

She nodded.

He helped her up, brushed her knees and hands, then got her settled in the black rubber seat.

"Thank you."

He shrugged. "No biggie."

She leapt from the seat to give him a hug.

Once she'd returned to the swing, Maisey noticed his cheeks had turned pink and though he was smiling again, he was also doing a lot of looking around. "You okay if I leave?"

"Uh huh, but do you have to?"

He nodded. "I got stuff to do."

"Okay. Well, thanks." She smiled up at him, but he was already gone.

Grinning, Maisey swang like forty whole, wonderful times before the bell rang for her class to go inside. Dillon never bothered her again. But Nash's smile sure did. Every time she thought about him, her tummy felt like butterflies were trapped inside, but then another sharper feeling took hold—like a dull squeeze that hurt.

Maisey had dozed off again, and woke to not only painful cramping, but black water sloshing and swirling around her ankles.

Was the boat sinking?

13

Nash figured they would have found civilization by now.

He killed the engine again to bail. This was the third time he'd followed the routine and though it was getting old, it sure beat the hell out of traversing the swamp on foot.

Maisey had been asleep for hours, and he was glad. She'd been through hell and no doubt needed the rest. For a while, he'd bunked with her, but it was impossible to fully relax with one hand on his Glock and both eyes on the water.

Kicking himself for dumping that GPS, he'd gone old school and followed the North Star whenever the tree canopy broke enough to see it. Of course, he'd had swamp survival training, but this closed-in shit was no *bueno*. He'd spent the last decade either training at Little Creek in Virginia or using that training in a desert.

Leaving all that gear and food had been stupid. Why had he done it?

Sheer panic over the welfare of the girl who'd always held a special place in his heart. Practically their whole childhood, she'd been getting into messes that he'd helped her out of. The thought of her being held captive by Vicente was bad enough, but toss in that other set of random thugs and he'd been out of his freakin' mind with worry—which he didn't do.

Had never done before losing his wife and baby.

Which is part of what prompted the beginning of the end of his military career, and even his split with Trident, Inc.

He bailed faster and faster while trying to make peace with the fact that somewhere along the way, his feelings for his family had robbed him of the ability to detach. He no longer saw events unfold with clinical precision. Kill or be killed. Not only had his own mortality come into play—fear for how Hope and his future son would manage without him—but fear for how he'd manage without them. When that worst case scenario had come true, the bottom of his world had fallen out from under him. He'd been left with no true north. Ironic, considering that was the path he had now been literally forced to follow.

"Nash?"

He stopped mid-bail to go to Maisey. "What's up?"

"Are we sinking?" The moonless night made visibility far less than ideal.

"Not at the moment. I've got us parked on a hammock. Our friends shot-up the hull pretty bad, and we're taking on water. I've been stopping to bail."

"You should have woken me. I would've helped." She hugged herself from the night's chill, then seemed to fuss with her position.

"Everything okay? You look uncomfortable."

"I am." She rubbed her lower back. "I've got some cramping, too, but it's probably no big deal."

He groaned. "I've got to get you out of here. If only I knew where *here* actually was. Vicente's place was thirty-six miles as the crow flies from Green Fork, but his land borders the Everglades. I thought we were on a main channel, but it petered out. We've passed a couple fishermen, but I'm hesitant to flag anyone down for fear of them having connections to Vicente."

"I'm sorry," she said softly.

"For what?"

"Everything. If I had done what you said back at Vicente's compound, we'd have already been safe."

"True, but don't blame yourself. These kinds of situations are highly fluid—and I'm not just talking about all the freakin' water in this boat."

"Ha ha. I know. But I can't help feeling responsible. I wish I'd never met Vicente."

"Yeah, but then you wouldn't have your baby." He eased alongside her on the vinyl bench seat, turning her back to him so he could rub her tight shoulders. "No matter what, your little boy is going to be worth it."

"Vicente was happy for a son." Her voice barely rose above the frogs and cicadas. "He needs someone to carry on his family name. It's an obsession."

That explained a lot.

"At first, I felt sorry for him, but the further along I got in my pregnancy, the more demanding he grew. He isolated me and then locked me in my room. Like that wasn't bad enough, lately, he's been even worse. Cuffing me in my bed, and having his private physician examine me at the house." She bowed her head. "I've been so naïve. I honestly believed that as long as I was pregnant, he would never hurt me. That if I did as he said, as soon as I had the baby, I could either get help or make him see reason. His actions didn't make sense. I loved him. I . . . was a fool."

"Hey . . ." Nash pulled her back against him, kissing the crown of her head, more determined than ever to see her and her baby safely through.

"Love makes everyone do crazy things. I know it did me. Once Hope told me she was carrying our baby, I became a different man. I didn't know I was capable of loving that hard. I loved those two so much that it became a liability. In the field, my every action was based on the likelihood of whether or not my team and I would make it out alive. No matter what, I had to survive for Hope and our future child. But when I heard they'd died in the fire, I lost it. I wanted to die—to be . . . with them." His throat was so tight, the admission barely escaped. But at last, his truth had come out. What had he been doing back in Jacksonville all these months? Essentially, trying to die, but being too much of a coward to properly do the job.

"Oh, Nash . . ." Her voice caught.

At some point while they'd talked, Nash had slipped his arms around her, resting his hands on her baby bump. She placed her smaller hands atop his, easing her fingers between his, and suddenly he was no longer alone, but once again part of a team. Like back in high school, Maisey and him against the world.

She raised his hands to her mouth, kissing the backs, and then turning them over to kiss his sensitive palms. She had no idea how much dirt Nash had on them—literally and figuratively. He tried drawing them away. But she held firm, refusing to let him go. "You're done dying, Nash. I selfishly need you to live. If only I'd accepted your proposal all those years ago, just think of how different—how much better—everything might be now."

"Yeah . . ." But in the same respect, if that meant never having met Hope, or watching his child grow inside her—virtually erasing them from his memory—that was the last thing he wanted to do. He'd vowed long ago that if he couldn't die and be with them, at the very least, he'd never be with another woman.

No matter how glad Nash was to be reunited with Maisey, he had no intention of breaking that vow.

14

Maisey woke from a deep, dreamless sleep to find herself still cradled in Nash's strong arms, with the sun peeking over the horizon. They faced a vast sawgrass prairie. After having spent hours breaking free of the tangled jungle, so much open space felt exhilarating. It didn't matter that they still might be miles from civilization. That also meant they were most likely miles from Vicente and those other horrible men.

She held her breath through another cramp, reassuring herself that it was normal. That it hurt less than the ones she'd had last night.

Finding Nash again changed everything. Being with him made her feel like that grinning schoolgirl he'd rescued by the swings. With him by her side, she could soar to impossible heights. Nothing could bring her down.

In the night, he'd wanted to push forward, but she'd fought him. They needed rest, and so he'd let the back down on the bench seat, forming a surprisingly comfortable bed. Nash piled three life jackets atop one another to make himself a pillow, and Maisey used his chest. The air had still been stagnant and hot, and the bugs ridiculous, but secure against him, none of that mattered. She blocked everything but how safe and precious he made her feel.

The night they'd first made love had been the same.

Looking back on it, their union had been such a high school cliché, but she wasn't complaining.

Stroking the coarse hair on Nash's forearms, Maisey closed her eyes, letting the sun warm her face, letting memories take hold of the present.

"Sure about this?" Nash cupped her face with his hands, brushing her bottom lip with his thumb.

Maisey nodded. They stood outside their room—lucky 777—at the Holiday Inn where they'd danced the night away at their junior prom. Her mom thought she was spending the night in the suite Maisey had chipped in on with a bunch of her girlfriends from choir. She'd never before lied to her mom and felt terrible about doing it now, but obviously not bad enough to step away from the guy she loved.

He lowered his lips to hers, still holding her face, kissing her as if she were a fragile, precious flower.

She kissed him back harder.

The two of them had been together forever. Officially, since he'd asked her to be his girl on Valentine's Day when they'd been in eighth grade. They'd fooled around a lot over the years, and honestly Maisey was hungry—starving—for more.

Giggling, high on the vodka her friend, Delia, had snuck into the dance in a pink flask, Maisey took the card key from Nash's back pocket and slipped it in the lock. The light flashed from red to green. She opened the door with one hand and grabbed Nash's arm with the other. "You brought the condom, right?"

"Yeah. I got a jumbo pack in case we wanna do it all night long."

"You're crazy," she teased, using his tie to pull him toward her while the door slammed closed. "Oops. I didn't know it would shut that hard."

"Doesn't matter." They fell back into another kiss.

The hotel was new and according to the manager, they were "still working out the kinks", which was why the prom committee had been able to afford the ballroom. It was super fancy with swirl-patterned carpet and massive crystal chandeliers. Their private room was equally as nice. They hadn't turned lights on, but outside their seventh-floor window, all of Jacksonville twinkled.

"How do you want to do this?" Nash asked.

"I don't know. You're the guy. I thought you'd figure it out?"

"Duh. Like I know where to stick it, but do you want it on the bed or the sofa or what?" He looked as stressed as he'd

been the first time they'd taken their ACTs.

"Could you relax? This is supposed to be fun."

"I know. Sorry, but the room ended up costing like fifty bucks more than planned, and the front desk guy was all pissy 'cause I didn't have a credit card."

"It's okay. None of that matters. I know you're saving for college, so I'll split the money with you. I want tonight to be special. Don't you?"

"Well, yeah. Why else would we be here?"

"Exactly. So to answer your question, I think we should take a bubble bath together, and then do it on the bed. Sound like a plan?"

"I'm down."

"Good." She fumbled in the bathroom to turn on the light.

It was a beautiful space with fancy gold striped wallpaper and a marble countertop with the sink a square bowl that rested on top. The tub was oversized and perfectly white. The house she shared with her mom didn't have a tub, so the only place she ever got to have a bath was at her grandma's. Maisey didn't see her all that often, so this was a big deal. Plus, her grandmother's tub was pink and not very big and even though she used lots of bubbles, she could always still smell her grandmother's Bengay.

Nash's mom had offered to let her use their tub, but Maisey had been too shy.

She turned on the taps, adjusting the water so it was nice and warm.

She reached for the bottle of hotel shampoo to add, but

then Nash said, "Wait."

He left the bathroom, and came back a minute later with a big, pink bottle of bubble bath champagne. "Thought you'd like this."

"I love it!" Grinning, she practically threw herself against him. "I love you."

"Love you, too."

Maisey poured in a bunch of the strawberry-scented pink liquid, then they kissed some more before taking off their clothes.

It was funny, they'd seen parts of each other naked, but never all at the same time. Once Nash stripped down to his boxers and Maisey stood in her pink bra and panties, she wasn't sure what to do next. Did she go all stripper and gyrate and stuff? Or would he take her stuff off? Was she supposed to remove his underwear? Who knew sex was so confusing?

"You're, ah, really hot." While staring at her boobs, Nash's cheeks turned red.

"Thanks." She crossed her arms. "So are you."

The water was getting pretty high. Bubbles toppled over the tub and onto the white marble-tile floor.

"Guess we should turn that off?" he said.

"Probs."

They both knew the simple task needed to be done, yet neither moved—at least until a huge sheet of bubbles avalanched onto Maisey's freshly-manicured toes.

Nash bolted into action, cutting off the water, then reaching low to pull up the stopper.

When he stood, and once again faced her, she gasped and covered her gaping mouth with her hands. "Look at your . . ."

His hard thingee had sprung free of his boxers, and stuck out straight.

"Geez . . ." He turned his back to her and she watched in the mirror while he tried shoving it back in. It didn't want to go.

"Nash, stop."

"What? It's not like I can help it."

"Did I say I wanted you to?" Maisey walked around him, and touched it, curious to finally see what she'd been holding and tugging and caressing all these years. Lots of times she'd felt it in the dark front seat of his old truck, but never seen it out and proud. She cupped her hands around him, surprised by how smooth and hot it was.

She knelt, and out of curiosity, licked the tip. It tasted salty.

"Jesus, Mais . . ." He lurched backwards. "You can't go doing stuff like that."

"Why not?"

"Because I'm supposed to do that to you."

"Then why don't you?"

"Here? In the bathroom."

"Why not? Chicken?" She smiled, knowing that like her, he never backed down from a challenge. "The whole place is brand new. Just think, we'll be the first ones who ever do it in here." She took two thick, white towels and stretched them across the floor before settling onto them. Between her legs felt wetter than the tub. She felt hot and dirty, but didn't care.

All she could think about was how she suddenly wanted his mouth everywhere.

He tugged off his boxers, then leaned over her for another kiss, and that first brush of his bare body against hers was electric. Sure, they'd kissed lots of times in their bathing suits at the neighborhood pool, but this was different. She had goose bumps.

"Cold?"

"Hot. Very hot." Maisey had read the line in one of Delia's Cosmos.

She pulled his head down to her chest, and he kissed the crowns of her boobs that were practically popping out of her bra. Her body sent signals she wasn't sure how to read. Her downstairs hummed and she pressed her legs together, dying for friction. Delia bragged about how she touched herself all the time, but Maisey never had. The few times she'd tried, the cat jumped on her bed.

The thought made her giggle.

"What's wrong?" Nash asked. "Doesn't this feel good?"

Maisey closed her eyes. "It feels great, babe."

He swept his kisses lower and lower until reaching the apex of her legs.

Excitement bubbled in her throat and she wasn't sure what to do with her hands. She rested them on her belly, but then Nash nudged her thighs apart and was pressing hot, wet open-mouthed kisses to her inner thighs. She felt the oddest, hungry yearning for more, and raised her hips up to meet his mouth. He ran the tip of his tongue along her panty line, and then moved the thin, silky fabric aside, to kiss her lower lips.

93

It wasn't enough—not nearly enough.

She tried wriggling free of her panties, but they weren't coming off.

He helped and once they finally passed her ankles, Nash flung them under the sink. Maisey should have gone with the G-string like Delia said. Then, Nash could have ripped them off like guys did in movies.

With him back between her legs, her body quivered with a strange need. She was so wet down there, and she was embarrassed he might see, but then he was pushing her legs apart and kissing her and licking her in places where no one had ever been, and she couldn't breathe.

The sensation of the tip of his tongue flicking against what could only be her clit was beyond belief good. Like behind her closed eyes, a kaleidoscope of color and light warred with the steadily rising pressure. He'd found her hole and pressed his tongue in deep, establishing a rhythm that made her wild.

Maisey bucked with his each thrust. Moans left her throat in a husky voice she no longer recognized.

Was this even real?

She slid her fingers into his hair, pulling until she rode the crest of a wave only to fall and fall until he was catching her.

"I-I have to get a condom," he said on a ragged breath.

"No. Don't leave me. I'll be fine."

He eased up the length of her body and she felt his thingee pressing against her thigh. When he kissed her, she tasted herself on his tongue which only made her hotter and wetter and more determined than ever to get him inside her now.

She fumbled for him, helping him find her hole.

"Sure?" he again asked.

She again nodded.

And then he was easing inside. She was so wet and ready, she didn't think it would hurt, but it did. She cried out.

"Want me to stop?" He drew back.

"No. Please . . ." Please what, she didn't know. Just that she needed him inside her, finishing what they'd begun.

He plunged back in, and this time, she felt a subtle shift of her body welcoming him inside. She swelled for him and raked her fingertips up his back. She arched up to meet his every thrust, and when he exploded inside her, and then shuddered, she held him close, never wanting the magic to end.

Her whole world seemed sharper.

She felt the cold marble floor seeping through the towels onto her back. She smelled the strawberry bubbles and heard a steady drip from the tub faucet. Most of all, with him still deep inside her, she felt his heart beating against hers.

They were connected. They were one.

"I came inside you," he said.

"It's okay."

"What if you get pregnant?"

"That would be okay, too. We'll get married and buy a sweet little house. We'll be so happy with our baby boy or girl."

He pushed off of her to stare deep into her eyes. "Is that what you want?"

"Uh huh."

"Me, too."

They kissed again, and then she started to cry. Not because she was sad, but because she was so incredibly, Willy-Wonka happy.

"Hey, sleepyhead. We've gotta get this show on the road."

Maisey was slow to wake, but then she opened her eyes to see Nash's dear face and it didn't matter that she was back in a swamp, covered in bug bites and hungrier and dirtier than she'd ever been. She didn't care that bad guys were looking to shoot them, and her latest cramp hurt worse. As long as she and Nash were together, everything would be okay.

"Do you remember junior prom?" She sat up so she could face him, loving that his cheeks blushed red.

"Kinda hard to forget."

She giggled. "I know, right? But it was good. That was the perfect night."

He swatted a mosquito. "It was a great time, but let's skip memory lane and get you and the baby to a doctor."

"Agreed." Another cramp hit. This one hard enough to steal her breath. She had to keep telling herself it was no big deal, because no way was she having this baby in a swamp. "But we had fun, right?"

After kissing her forehead, he said, "You were amazing."

Though she craved more—like a kiss to her lips—she pushed herself upright, then gave him a corny salute. "Aye-aye, captain." She waved to the front of the boat toward a sandy stretch of shore. "Let me visit the ladies room and we'll set sail."

He helped her waddle over the craft's low side hull, then delivered a stern lecture on staying within his view, and not getting too close to the water's edge.

Her nightgown was a mess, and without a tree to lean against, she couldn't remove her panties without losing balance. "Nash? Could I get a little help?"

He'd been fiddling with the boat's engine, but in seconds returned to her side. "What's up?"

"This is embarrassing, but I'm too big to get my . . ." She gestured lower. "You know, *off*, so I can pee."

"Oh. *Ooooh*." He was once again blushing through his stubble. Ever the gentleman, he knelt beside her, looking away while tugging down her panties. If they'd been anywhere else, she'd have been all over him—especially, after reliving their first steamy time. Her memories were so vivid, the brush of his knuckles against her outer thighs was almost enough to make her come.

Her baby books had talked about some women

being *needy* right before delivery, and how sex could even speed things along during labor, but this was ridiculous.

"Go ahead and do your thing." He turned his back to her, but the sight of him holding her hot pink panties made her smile. "I'll wait."

How awkward would it be having him help tug them back on? She'd rather go commando.

The day's temp was already rising, and the sandy-bottomed water around the hammock was crystal clear. She'd for sure see any critter swimming toward her. Feeling about as fresh as a two-day-old bologna sandwich left in a baggie on the seat of a car, she strolled into the water, loving the instant cool.

"What are you doing?" Nash asked. "On land, we at least have a fighting chance against gators, but not with you in the water."

"Relax, *Mom*. I'm fine." Able to see at least twenty feet ahead, she sloshed out to her knees and splashed water onto her legs, arms and chest. It felt so refreshing that she went deeper, washing her face. The water made her huge belly buoyant. The relief on her lower back practically made her purr.

"Seriously, get back to shore. We need to get going."

"Okay. Give me a few more minutes."

"Maisey, we—what the—*shit*!"

She turned to see what had Nash so cranky, then screamed.

15

Holy hell . . . Nash had heard Burmese pythons were getting to be a nuisance in the Everglades, but this was ridiculous. A snake at least fifteen feet long had latched onto his left calf and now squeezed the shit out of both legs and was still climbing. He tried wrenching him off, but the massive fucker was still climbing.

Nash reached for the knife he kept strapped on his utility belt, but the snake had already covered it.

Knocked off balance, Nash fell.

"Maisey, calm down, get to the boat, and grab the machete that's back by engine."

"*Ohmygod*!" Wide-eyed and borderline hysterical, she made him proud by pulling herself together and getting to the boat. She struggled getting over the squat side hull, but eventually made it.

The pain and pressure the snake applied was incredible.

If Maisey couldn't make it back, how long did he have until he could no longer breathe? Heart pounding in his ears, never had Nash felt less a man.

He shoved and pushed and tried kicking, but somehow the snake was still climbing higher. His chest felt tight and his head throbbed.

Hurry, Mais . . .

His vision blurred, and he was hotter than hot. Sweat rained from his forehead, beading into his eyes. He tried wiping them, but his arms no longer worked. Was this the end?

Suddenly, she was there. Crying out, slashing at the snake's gesticulating coils. "Hold on, Nash. Don't you dare die . . ."

He couldn't breathe. The snake worked his rib cage, squeezing out his last breath. He wanted to answer Maisey, to tell her how much he cared.

"Nash! Open your eyes and fight! I need you!" she cried while slashing and then, with them both covered in bloody snake parts and looking like victims of a psycho slasher movie, he dragged in a breath and his lungs were once again filled with air instead of panic. His mind sharpened and his arms were strong enough to push free of the creature's limp coils.

Holy shit . . . Still dazed, Nash pushed himself

upright.

"You're okay . . ." Maisey was hugging him and crying and when he took her into his arms, it was with newfound awe.

"Do you realize you took on a fifteen-foot snake and won?"

"I was so scared for you."

"That makes two of us." Nash managed a laugh. "I was so worried about alligators that it never occurred to me to worry about man-eating snakes."

"Come on," she took his hand, leading him toward the water. "Let's get cleaned off."

His legs wobbled, and his pride fell another dozen notches as he was forced to concede that if his pregnant first love hadn't been holding him up, he would have fallen.

She helped him sit on the sandy bottom, then washed him as if he were a child. She hummed an ethereal tune and his shoulders sagged as he surrendered to her and the moment, grateful to be alive.

"I'm stupid off my game," he noted.

"Hush. You're fine."

"No. For real, I'm supposed to be saving you." He sighed.

"You have—about a dozen times. Now, drop it. You're still a big, tough guy, and I still love . . . you." She'd washed his face and now dropped to her knees, kissing his forehead and cheeks and nose. "I've always loved you."

Nash closed his eyes, wanting to return her beautiful sentiment, knowing he should love her, and once had deeply. But he couldn't. Not anymore. He was badly broken, and if this recent turn of events hadn't proven that to her, nothing would.

"Nash?" She raised his chin. "Say something— anything." Her fathomless blue eyes begged, *please*.

"We should get going."

Still staring and with tears welling, she nodded.

"Let's keep heading north. We'll have to eventually hit I-75."

"Great plan." She no longer met his gaze and more than he'd been scared of once again losing himself to her, he was that much more afraid of never again having her. Without his wife, he'd felt adrift, but here in this godforsaken swamp, he'd begun to think he might again have a reason for life. A life that, in a perfect world, might begin and end with Maisey.

She struggled upright and swam to the boat, once again fighting to drag herself aboard. Back in high school, Nash's best friend, Todd, had a ski boat they'd take out on weekends. He'd been too broke to buy a swim ladder, so they'd all perfected the art of climbing over the side. Apparently, Maisey hadn't lost her touch. Was there anything the woman couldn't do?

Nash was more impressed with her than ever— not that the fact changed anything. "Aw, Mais, wait . .

."

The snake bite in his calf hurt like a sonofabitch, but the rest of him seemed to be in working order. He made it to the boat in time to hold out his hands, offering to help her the rest of the way to her seat.

Stoney eyed, she silently rejected his offer.

"You know I love you, Mais—like family." *I'm sorry, but that's all I'm capable of for now. Maybe ever.* After what she'd been through, she deserved more.

"Whatever. Can we go?"

He opened his mouth to explain, but what was the point? She was pissed, and he had no eloquent way to tell her his heart would forever belong to a dead woman.

Nash tried starting the engine, but got nothing.

No *ruh*, *ruh*, *ruh*. No ticking. Nada.

Shit.

"Nash . . . Could you please come here? I-I think we have a problem."

"Damn straight we do." He tried the motor again. "This sucker's dead. But what the hell? It worked fine when I shut it off."

"Nash, please . . ."

"I know you're ready to get started." He'd already made his way to the back of the boat to check battery connections. "I'm working as fast as I can."

"This isn't about the stupid engine!" Her shrieked tone was loud enough to roust the seagull who'd landed atop the airboat's fan into flight.

"Then what's the problem?" In no mood for a confrontation about his *feelings*, Nash stormed past the bench seats to her. "From where I'm standing, a busted engine is kind of a huge problem."

"Not as big as this." She pointed to the pool of yellowish liquid at her feet.

"Are you hurt?" *I'm a dick*. "What happened? Did you cut yourself climbing onto the boat?"

"Worse." She hugged her huge belly. "I think my water broke."

16

"Wait—what does that even mean?" Nash asked. "Like I get what the fluid is, but your water only breaks when you're about to deliver, right?"

Maisey nodded. "Usually in twenty-four hours. But I'm only at thirty-two weeks. My baby's too small. Plus, because of a risk of infection, I'm not supposed to even bathe, so I'm guessing a swamp walk is a bad idea."

"Lord . . ." He raked his hands through his hair. "Yeah, I remember Hope being a wreck because she was always afraid hers would break at the grocery store. The doctor told her most women have theirs break during delivery."

"Perfect. But I don't have a doctor—just you."

Honestly, she'd have rather been alone. Confessing her love for him, only to be told that he essentially loved her like a sister had come as quite a blow. It shouldn't have. She'd long ago passed on her chance to be with him, but the vivid dreams she'd been having told another story. Reliving their first time had brought everything rushing back. He'd been her rock, supporting her through each of life's blows. It hadn't mattered if she'd flunked a geometry test or her car wouldn't start or her mom caught her dad cheating again. Regardless of the circumstance, Nash was always there—until he wasn't. And she'd been forced to rely on herself. It hadn't been an easy transition, but she'd done it and thought herself better off having learned the skills. Then Vicente had come along, and she'd leaned on him. Why was she now once again turning over her power to Nash? It made no sense.

It does if you never stopped loving him.

She bit her lip through the rising pain of what she now knew wasn't a cramp, but a contraction, then glanced up to find Nash staring. "On the plus side," he said, "I've been to a lot of places where having babies in grass huts is normal, so I know we theoretically can do this. It's not ideal that your little guy is small, but we've got this. Don't worry, okay?"

"Sure." Easier said than done.

"Sit tight. I'm going to work on the engine. Hopefully, it's an easy fix—a loose wire or spark plug."

Whatever. She was done. Allowing herself to be wrapped in the fantasy of what she and Nash once shared had been a mistake. She'd soon be a single mom, which meant she no longer had the luxury of lingering in the past when, like it or not, she was barreling toward her future.

A low humming on the horizon caught her attention. A boat?

Maisey grunted, pushing to her feet, shading her eyes from the already bright sun. An ancient Wellcraft was barely visible, but coming closer.

"Hey! Hey!" She crossed her arms over her head, hoping to draw the driver's attention.

"What the hell are you doing?" Nash practically ambushed her, dragging down her arms, and jerking her beside him.

"Unlike you, I'm getting us rescued." She struggled free.

"You don't even know who that is," he said when the boat came close enough for them to clearly identify a man and woman on board. "They could have ties to Vicente."

"Hey!" Freed from Nash's hold, Maisey waved all the harder. "Over here! Help!"

"Are you crazy?" He fought her again. "I know you're pissed, but you're not being smart."

The boat turned in their direction.

"Thank God." Relief shimmered through her in

dizzying waves. Assuming these undoubtedly nice locals knew their way around the swamp, her baby would be born in a safe, snake-free environment.

"Take this." He handed her a sheathed knife. "Keep it hidden in case things go bad." He tucked a pistol in the waistband of his pants, drawing his shirt over it. He also had two knives and a second gun in his cargo pants' thigh pocket.

"Look at them," she said with the family fishing boat now in full view. An elderly couple sat beneath a shaded canopy. Each held a bottled sweet tea. A bag of Ruffles potato chips rested on the bench seat between them. An assortment of fishing poles, coolers and crab pots littered the front of the boat. Hip waders and life jackets had been mounded on the back.

"Ahoy," the white-bearded man said with a friendly wave. He reminded Maisey of Santa. "You having engine trouble?"

"Yessir," Nash stepped in front of her. Maybe he thought Santa and plump, smiley Mrs. Claus might launch a surprise marshmallow gun attack? For the first time since leaving Vicente's compound, Maisey dared exhale. Everything truly would be all right. "Probably the battery. Mind giving us a jump?"

"I'll do you one better—how about a tow back to our dock, then you can work at your leisure on fixing the problem. Mother, here, will fix us a nice—"

"Harvey, hush. Look at that poor girl. Can't you

see she's miserable and about to pop?" The elderly woman stood, offering Maisey her hand to help ease the transfer to their boat.

"I'm still not sure this is a good idea," Nash said under his breath. "Let me check them out first."

"Stop." Maisey was done with his mission. While she appreciated his rescue more than he could ever know, for now she needed this darkness behind her at least long enough to welcome her innocent baby into the world. She had no illusions that Vicente wouldn't still move heaven and earth to find her, but for this brief window in time, all was right in the world.

The adorable saviors brought their boat close, and sheer adrenaline-fueled joy helped Maisey safely aboard.

Nash reluctantly followed.

Introductions were made and Maisey admitted her water had broke, so she needed medical assistance ASAP.

"Since y'all are in a hurry," Harvey said, "how about I bring Nash back around for your boat later? You know, once the missus and baby are settled."

"That'd be great. Thanks." Nash shook the man's hand, but his rigid posture told Maisey he was nowhere near relaxed.

"You poor thing," the kindly woman offered Maisey her seat beside the captain. "I mean no disrespect, but you look a mess. Been out here long?"

Maisey nodded. "Do you have any bottled water?"

"Where are my manners?" Mildred not only doled out chilled waters, but ham and cheese sandwiches, deviled eggs and chips.

"Thank you," Maisey managed between frantic bites. "My baby books said I wouldn't be hungry close to delivery, but they lied." Knowing they'd had nothing, she'd put hunger and thirst from her mind, but now both matters were front and center. "It's been a while since our last meal."

"What exactly were y'all doing out here?" Harvey asked from behind the craft's steering column.

"Fishing," Nash said.

"Sightseeing," Maisey stupidly said over him.

"Judging by your nightie," Mildred said to Maisey with an exaggerated wink, "I figured you two were newlyweds, out for a day of hanky-panky."

"We tossed in a bit of that, too." Nash finished his water, then started on his sandwich.

Harvey fired up the engine with a chuckle. "I always say the worst day fishing is better than the best day working. Throw in some good, old-fashioned necking and you've got a fine morning indeed."

"Oh, for heaven's sake," Mildred lurched forward to give her man a good-natured swat. "Just because your mind lives in the gutter, doesn't mean you have to share the filth that comes out."

ROGUE

The two bickered above the engine's steady hum.

Maisey leaned back, beyond thankful. Having Mildred and Harvey find them was nothing short of a heaven-sent miracle. Her mind struggled to switch gears from the rapid transition from depths of despair to rescue.

Rehydrated, with food in her tummy, she rode out the latest contraction like a champ, breathing along with the rise and swell, reassuring herself that this nightmare would soon be over. As soon as she safely delivered her baby, she'd report Vicente to authorities, they'd pick him up and haul him off to a cell, and then she and Nash could be on their way to Jacksonville for a nice, long visit with their moms—not that they'd be together past then. He'd made his feelings for her—or rather, lack thereof—clear.

And honestly? If she hadn't been under constant attack by gun-toting bad guys, alligators, snakes or mosquitoes, she never would have blurted that nonsense about love.

If the topic was ever again broached, she'd plead temporary insanity.

A little under an hour later, Harvey pulled the boat into a charming, rustic wooden dock complete with a tin roof, screened fish-cleaning station, and flower boxes overflowing with sweet-smelling red-and-white petunias.

Exhaustion clung to Maisey, bearing down on

111

her shoulders and tight neck.

The latest contraction had teeth, and she struggled to keep her cool.

"Oh dear," Mildred took one look at Maisey and frowned. "Looks like our little momma's not doing so well. Harvey, as soon as the boat's tied, let's get our girl to the guest bed. I have a feeling her little one will be with us sooner as opposed to later."

"Agreed," Harvey said. "She is looking a bit green around her gills."

"I'll help." The moment Harvey killed the engine, Nash sprung to action, tying off the boat while their host retrieved a four-wheeler.

Mildred had already dashed for the house to call 9-1-1.

Nash scooped Maisey into his arms, carrying her to the vehicle's wagon-style trailer.

She rested her cheek against his shoulder. Overriding the sweat and the swamp's musk was the familiar scent of him. The closer her contractions grew, the more helpless Maisey felt and the more she realized how much she needed her old friend.

"Hang in there." He set her onto the cool metal trailer's bed. His touch was so gentle, so kind, the concern in his gaze so genuine, that she knew no matter what he'd said about having no feelings for her, he'd lied. Or maybe he'd said he did have feelings for her, but they were strictly platonic? She couldn't be sure. The closer and harder contractions struck, the more muddied her thoughts grew.

Suddenly that sandwich and three deviled eggs didn't seem like all that great of an idea. All at once Maisey was nauseous, yet struggling for air during the agonizing rise of her latest contraction.

"I'm scared." She grappled for Nash's hand. "Please, don't leave me."

"Never," he assured with a tender kiss to her forehead.

"Ready to get this little lady to a proper bed?" Harvey asked from behind the wheel.

"Absolutely."

After the initial jolt of Harvey launching the vehicle into motion, he drove smoothly down a hard-packed sand lane lined with slash pines.

When the next contraction hit, Maisey bit her lower lip to keep from crying out. The pain was beyond intense. Her baby was coming—*soon*.

"Almost there," Harvey said.

Nash jogged alongside the cart. If he had lingering effects from the snake bite, he sure didn't show it.

Maisey closed her eyes, forcing deep breaths while riding out what now felt like constant pain-filled waves. "I-I need to push!"

"Not yet, babe. Let's get you in a bed, then you can push all you want, okay?"

She nodded, or maybe rocked her head side-to-side. She couldn't be sure of anything other than the fact that it wouldn't be long until she held her son in her arms.

Harvey parked the vehicle next to the screened back porch of an Airstream trailer that had been joined with a cabin. The structure may have been unconventional, but it beat the heck out of having her baby in the heart of the swamp. Maisey was beyond grateful that Harvey and Mildred had come along when they did.

Nash stooped to heft her back into his arms.

"This way," Harvey held open the porch door. "Then through the kitchen and down the hall. The guest room is the third door on your right."

"Thanks." He edged sideways to fit her through.

Maisey caught flashes of her surroundings—a darling vintage tea cup collection and a shelf lined with antique Teddy bears. Plush Oriental rugs and shabby chic overstuffed furnishings with sherbet-toned slipcovers. The whole place smelled clean and fresh with a hint of lemon. She'd hit the jackpot in rescuers.

"Right in here," Mildred waved from the end of the hall. "I called for an ambulance, but as far out as we are, it could take over an hour."

Maisey gritted her teeth through her latest contraction. "I-I can't wait that long."

"No worries, dear . . ." Mildred tossed back a pink floral quilt on a white-wrought iron bed, directing Nash to place Maisey atop pink sheets. The walls were painted a darker rose. Built-in bookshelves framed a window seat decked out in floral chintz curtains and pillows. Sunshine pooled at the foot of the bed and for whatever odd reason, Maisey's emotions got the better of her. What a wondrous change of luck to have been transported from a nightmare to this feminine haven. "You go right ahead and have your baby now."

"I-I can't!" Groaning through a particularly rough contraction, Maisey shook my head. "Not here."

"Whyever not?" The kindly innkeeper propped Maisey by planting four pillows behind her back.

"It's too nice. I don't want to ruin your pretty room."

While Maisey cried, Mildred patted her shoulder. "Don't you worry about a thing. Sheets can be washed, but if it makes you feel better, I've got bed pads left from when Harvey had gallbladder surgery. How about I pop a few of those under you?"

"Yes, please."

"Is there anything I can do?" Nash eased his fingers between hers. A concerned crease had taken up residence between his eyebrows.

Maisey shook her head, struggling for her next breath as the pain rose into an even higher wave.

A phone rang on the nightstand. A glance in that direction confused her, then struck terror in her soul. *No.* This couldn't possibly be . . .

The caller ID read: *Rodriguez, Intl.*

Vicente's sham import company name that he used for money laundering. Maisey's pulse went berserk, hammering to a painful degree.

How had her fake husband found these people? How could they have gone along with whatever bribe he'd offered? How could they live with themselves, knowing once they turned them over, Maisey's ex wanted them killed?

"Harvey, love," Mildred coaxed another pillow beneath Maisey's head. "Could you please be a dear and handle that call. I want our momma as comfy as possible."

Maisey wanted to rail at her to get away. As if childbirth wasn't enough on her plate, she now had to contend with psycho granny and her Santa sidekick.

"Absolutely, dear." He took the receiver from its charge stand. "I'll answer in the other room, so as not to disturb you nesting hens. Nash, since the ladies have this under control, care to join me in a pre-celebration round of bourbon?"

No! Don't leave me. Maisey's contraction was so strong, she could hardly think, let alone speak. How did she let Nash know he'd been right about these two?

"Thanks for the kind offer, Harvey. It's a little early to be drinking, but I could use a restroom."

Maisey waved to him, but he stood with his

back to her, and couldn't see. *Arrrgggghhh*. She gritted her teeth through the crest of the latest wave.

"I'll bet you do, son. Follow me, and I'll point you in the right direction."

"Nash, no!"

"What's wrong?" He turned to her. His tender smile meant the world, but all the smiles in the world wouldn't save them from this latest mess of her making. "Besides the obvious?"

"I-I . . ." It was a struggle to find the right words. She couldn't hear over her haywire pulse and though she felt sticky from sweat, her body wouldn't stop shivering. Was she in shock? "I need you."

"I'm here, babe—not going anywhere."

"I need to take this call." Harvey wagged the phone. "Nash, come find me when you're ready."

"Will do."

"Mildred," Maisey said between ragged breaths, "please, could I have water?"

"Of course, dear. Nash," she patted his shoulder, "make sure our little momma doesn't go anywhere."

The second she was out of earshot, Maisey whispered, "W-we have to go . . ."

17

"What do you mean? Maisey, you're not in the condition to go to the bathroom, let alone outside." Could pain be making her delirious?

"Y-you were right. Mildred and Harvey—they're *bad.*"

"How? I know I had reservations at first, but they seem harmless enough."

"*Nooo.*" Teeth clenched, she thrashed her head side-to-side. "Vicente was on the phone. Saw it on the caller ID."

Shit. "Okay, I know you're ready to push, but try keeping that baby in. I'm going to leave you for a minute—tops. But I *will* be back." Nash smoothed the hair back from her fevered forehead. Why the hell couldn't he keep his head in the game? He'd been so worried about Maisey safely delivering her baby that he'd forgotten his primary goal wasn't to be her doctor, but her protector. "Can you stay tough for me?"

Tears streaming down her flushed cheeks, she nodded.

"Awesome. Sit tight." Nash bolted into the hall, but then slowed, not wanting to tip Mildred and Harvey off to the fact that they were in on their twisted con.

Nash was all manner of pissed—not only with himself, but them. How much was the bounty Vicente had placed on their heads?

He didn't have a long wait to find out. At the end of the hall, he overheard them softy talking.

"Fifty. Thousand. Dollars." Mildred giggled. The tone creeped Nash the hell out. "Can you imagine? Of course, we want to put in the pool, but do you think we could manage a new boat, too?"

"I don't see why not? At least one that'll be new to us," Harvey added with his usual chuckle.

The greedy duo turned Nash's stomach.

As did the thought that while poor Maisey was in pain, they were counting the coins they stood to make from her suffering—not that they were responsible for her labor pains, but they sure as hell would be for whatever twisted scenario Vicente would subject her to.

A right turn veered Nash toward a homey living

room.

Sofa. Two chairs. TV.

Since he couldn't pop off Santa and Mrs. Claus, he at least needed something to restrain the soon to be not-so-happy couple. Eyeing multiple electronics' cords tangled behind the TV, Nash used his favorite knife to slice clean through from the backs of a VCR, DVD, sound bar, and the TV. Once they'd all been cut from the respective sources, he yanked them from a power strip.

Hearing Maisey moan from the bedroom propelled Nash forward at an ever-increasing speed. If Mildred and Harvey's road was anything like most of the others around here, there were dozens of isolated off-shoots where he could hide the truck he'd soon borrow from their hosts long enough for Maisey to have her baby, then rocket her to a Miami hospital. Honestly, he feared they'd need to go that far to escape Vicente's apparently considerable influence.

While Mildred and Harvey chatted about going on a nice, long Caribbean cruise, Nash shredded a pink-striped throw pillow into strips long enough to serve as excellent gags.

He stowed his knife, then slipped the cords through belt loops and shoved the rags into his front pocket. He crept behind Harvey—still out of view from his wife—mentally preparing himself for taking down the senior citizen who probably had been a decent guy until being faced with a moral decision in which the prospect of easy, tax-free cash had won out over following the Golden Rule.

Lightning fast, Nash reached his forearm around Harvey's neck, squeezing him in a rear naked choke that in ten seconds temporarily cut off blood flow from the carotid arteries to the brain.

While Harvey slumped lifeless in his chair, Mildred screamed.

"You killed him!" she said on the heels of a wail. "After all we did for you and your hussy, you killed him!"

"He'll come out of this fine. You, on the other hand . . ." While restraining Harvey to his kitchen table chair, then gagging him, Nash gave her the special smile he usually reserved for Al Qaeda.

"Oh, God . . ." She shrunk against the kitchen counter. "Please, don't kill me! We have a daughter in Boca!"

"Lady, you've got about three seconds to tell me how long it'll be before Vicente or one of his men show up."

"I-I don't know what you're talking about." She gripped the yellow laminate counter so hard her knuckles turned white.

"Lie." Nash stepped toward her, holding out the cords.

"He came by this morning—said a man kidnapped his poor, pregnant wife. Well, me and Harvey have heard enough gossip over the years to know Vicente's no saint, but he gives a *lot* of money to the community and keeps mostly to himself and never did hurt anyone, so—"

Nash snapped the cords. "Skip to the highlight reel. How long till he shows up?"

She gulped, then darted her gaze to a digital clock built into the back of the stove. "I'm guessing fifteen minutes."

"Perfect." Grasping her by her upper arms, he propelled her toward a slim door he hoped led to a utility closet. "Open it."

"Oh, God! You're going to kill me by making me drink bleach!"

Lord . . .

When she opened the door, he gave her a light shove inside. "Lay off the CSI."

"Help! Help!" she shrieked once he'd closed the door behind her, and wedged a chair beneath the knob. If she shoved hard enough, she could easily break through, but hopefully this would at least buy him time to find the keys to the red Chevy pickup parked outside.

Harvey started to wake from his nap and looked none too happy to see Nash pluck his keys from the rack mounted above the counter.

"Don't you worry," Nash said with an acid smile. "You can use your fifty thousand to buy a nice, new model."

Harvey fought against his restraints, but experience had taught Nash they'd hold. Mildred would free herself long before Harvey.

In the bedroom, Nash found Maisey even more miserable than before.

"I-I heard a scream . . ."

"If that's your way of asking me if I killed her—no. She and Harvey will both live to con another day." He jangled the truck keys. "Ready for a ride?"

Not waiting for her answer, he scooped her from the bed, dragging along the comforter.

Nash bumbled his way outside, got her settled in the truck that was thankfully unlocked, then made one more trip into the house to grab towels, a T-shirt and jeans, a case of bottled water, and all the food and miscellaneous supplies he could cram into a canvas shopping bag. If all went well, they wouldn't need any of this crap, but if he'd learned anything during his time with Maisey, it's that luck typically was not on their side.

Spying a cell phone next to a loaf of bread on the counter, he grabbed it and the bread.

Behind the truck's wheel, Nash gunned the engine and drove the truck hard down the sandy lane. He had no idea where Vicente and his men might be, or how soon they'd encounter them.

Maisey looked scary pale.

With every shred of his being, Nash wanted to

hold her hand and reassure her everything would be okay, but he didn't have that luxury. To maintain their current speed, he needed both hands on the wheel.

She moaned, and he hated himself a little more.

This stretch of road could be a quarter-mile or twenty. If Vicente or his men drove up on them here, they'd be screwed. Assuming they'd have them outgunned was a no-brainer. Their only hope was to make it to the main highway or a viable turn-off before they met.

When their current path T-boned into a paved highway, assuming Vicente would approach from the west, Nash headed east.

Maisey's breathing had turned shallow and her complexion was gray.

His stomach twisted.

Gun play, wild animals—that kind of stuff he could handle. Well, mostly, if he didn't count massive snakes.

"I-I have to push," Maisey said. Her weak voice barely carried over the engine as he pushed their speed to eighty.

"Hold tight, babe. We should meet up with the ambulance soon." Although considering Mildred's comment about how beloved Vicente was in these parts, Nash wouldn't be surprised if the local paramedics and cops were also on his payroll.

"No . . ." She slumped in the seat, parting her

legs. "I-I have to push. The baby's coming!"

He checked the rearview, and with the coast clear, slowed to veer onto a gated park road. Of course, the gate was padlocked, so he rammed it, promising to send an anonymous chunk of cash to the park system earmarked for repairs.

A few yards on the gate's other side, he parked the truck, hopped out, then dummy-locked the gate to throw off casual onlookers.

Back behind the wheel, with Maisey huffing and panting beside him, Nash drove a sandy, then muddy five miles until stumbling across an abandoned-looking ranger's cabin that he parked behind.

"Give me a sec, and with luck I might have found you a bed."

Her only answer was a moan.

He picked the back door lock, and stepped into a world time had forgotten.

For once, he was happy about federal budget cuts. It looked like they had this place to themselves—aside from the odd rodent or two.

Sure enough, there was a lone bed, so he brushed it off as best he could, then layered it in the towels he'd snatched from Mildred. Next, he carried in Maisey, resting her near the end of the sagging mattress.

Trying to remain clinical, he slipped more towels beneath her, then mounded the comforter behind her for a pillow.

After a quick trip to the truck for bottled water, he pulled over a small bench, parking it at the foot of the bed in case he needed it when the baby came.

For now, Nash rinsed his hands, then dampened a washcloth he'd found mixed with the towels. When he rested it on Maisey's forehead, she gifted him with a faint smile.

"Give me a sec," he said, beyond flustered when she bore down, "to research emergency childbirth."

"No—just hold me. *Please.*" Her pained and pleading expression gutted him. In that moment, Nash had never felt more helpless, yet more determined to see her baby's delivery safely through.

He wrapped his arm around her slight shoulders and held one of her hands. She squeezed tight enough to cut off his circulation, but he didn't care. Nothing mattered but bringing her whatever comfort he could.

"Remember back in the swamp?" he asked, "When you said you loved me, but I was a dick and said I didn't love you?"

"K-kinda hard to forget." She shook from the force of her latest push.

"Yeah . . . Well, I lied. I've always loved you, but since Hope died, everything's screwed up in my head." Tears stung his eyes, and he found himself hating Vicente more than ever—not merely for being certifiable, but for landing her in this situation. She deserved better than giving birth in a musty-smelling old shack. A long time ago, she'd been his world. He'd have done anything for her, and he still would. He'd harbored such resentment toward her for turning down his proposal that he'd been open to a new relationship with Hope, whom he'd met a couple years after BUD/S training.

"I could have told you that." She managed a teary laugh. "T-tell me about her."

"No way. We should focus on you."

"I'm sick of—*arrrgggghh*." She squeezed his hand still tighter. "It hurts, it hurts, it hurts!"

"Sorry. Lean into me." Nash tossed aside the comforter, repositioning himself to sit behind her like he'd seen guys do in Lamaze pamphlets. With her back against his chest, he felt her every shuddering effort. "Better?"

She nodded. "T-Tell me about her. I need a distraction."

"Okay . . ." Where did he begin? "She was different from you. Tall, corporate-career-focused, with freckles and red hair and the temper to go along with it. She was always yelling at me for leaving a trail of dirty clothes and dishes."

Maisey managed a laugh. "I like her."

"She wanted kids. Bad. She came from a big family—was the youngest of eight brothers and sisters, and all of them already had big families. Over holidays, they'd razz us about being slow in the baby-making department, so when she found out she was pregnant, I'd never seen her happier."

"*Arrrggghhh*!" She fought extra hard through her latest push. "H-How did you tell her family? Were they excited?"

"Over the moon." For a moment, Nash squeezed his eyes shut, recalling how Hope had wrapped her positive pregnancy test in a gift box for him. "For her parents, she'd had me help her fill a big box with pink and blue helium-filled balloons. It was close to their anniversary, and we wrapped it in silver-foil paper. When those balloons rose from the box, her mother shrieked, then burst into tears. It was a seriously great moment."

"I'll bet. Did—" She stopped talking to make a terrifying cry. "S-Something's happening!"

Nash shot into action, standing, then repositioning her, pushing the comforter back in place, then checking out the epicenter of action. "Holy crap, Mais. Your baby's crowning. Push, sweetie. He's almost here."

Perched on the edge of the bench he'd earlier placed at the foot of the bed, he cupped his hands over her knees, hoping his touch conveyed at least a small part of his affection. Their lackluster surroundings faded until all that remained was the two of them in this most sacred of moments.

"Push, sweetie. You can do this. You're almost done, and then you get to hold your little guy in your arms."

She nodded and cried and wrenched her face into a mask of concentration.

With each push, the baby's head escaped a fraction of an inch, and then with one last screaming, crying effort, the tiny precious infant practically tumbled into Nash's outstretched arms.

Nash was crying and Maisey was crying and he felt he should say something profound, but had no words.

And then he froze in terror. The baby wasn't breathing.

18

"Mais, he's not breathing. What should I do?" Adrenaline cleared Maisey's exhaustion long enough to recall a passage she'd read in one of her baby books. "He probably needs suction, but cradle his chest against the palm of your hand and give his back a light thump with the heel of your hand."

Nash did exactly as she'd advised and a second later, they were rewarded with her son's first cry.

She exhaled the terror trapped in her lungs and smiled. *I did it.*

Her son was officially, safely in her world.

Nash gently nestled her baby boy against her chest, then covered him with a clean towel. "You did good, momma."

"Thanks." Whereas moments earlier she'd been in agonized tears, now, she couldn't stop smiling. "That was intense."

"No kidding. What do you want to do about cutting his cord? I snatched Santa's phone. If I have a signal, want me to look it up online?"

She nodded. "Please."

"Will do." He rinsed his hands, then refreshed the washcloth with clean water. "Would you like to bathe him, or do you want me to?"

"I'm exhausted. Would it make me a horrible mom if I let you?"

"Not at all." His sad, sweet smile flip-flopped her stomach. "Plus, I'd be honored. Let me get a fire going, and I'll heat some water. Don't want him catching a chill."

"Sounds good." She closed her eyes, hugging her son. "Nash?"

"Yeah?"

Maisey opened her eyes in time to see him pause by the door. Maybe it was her relieved, happy glow making her view the world in rose-colored glasses, but even covered in swamp muck, bug bites and bruises, the man was beyond gorgeous. He used to be hers, but she'd given him away. She'd been a fool. "You didn't have to say you love me. I understand Hope was—still is—special to you."

"Let's get one thing straight." He left the door to approach her, and then pressed a kiss to her fore-

131

head. Her chest squeezed with raw emotion. Why hadn't he kissed her lips? "I didn't tell you out of a sense of obligation, but because I do—love you. It's complicated. What I feel for Hope is . . ."

"Unresolved?" she found the courage to ask. Obviously, understandably, he still loved his deceased wife. But would he always? Maisey couldn't help but wonder if she was setting herself up for yet another romance fail by falling for him all over again.

He winced. "Guess that's one way of looking at it."

Maisey's son stirred against her. *My son.* The phrase would never get old.

What was old? Being alone. Even when things had been good with Vicente, looking back on it, he'd never been one hundred percent focused on her—not like Nash once had been. Not like he currently was. But his presence was temporary.

As soon as they returned to town, she'd report Vicente to police, and hopefully settle into a satisfying routine in Jacksonville. Maybe she'd one day meet a man who attracted her and challenged her half as much as Nash. Maybe she wouldn't. Regardless, she had to make peace with that, because she no longer had the luxury of caring about only herself.

With Vicente, she'd made horrendous judgment calls, and that had to stop.

Nash was back. "Fire's made. I found an old rain-filled cistern so we have plenty of water. Harvey was even kind enough to leave a nice, big crab-boil pot in the back of his truck."

"That was thoughtful," she said with a winced smile.

"I know, right?" He winked. "Are you hungry? Thirsty?"

"Parched."

He delivered a bottled water, and helped her drink. "I did some quick studying up on our situation, and you should breastfeed as soon as you're ready. Plus, you should have delivered your placenta. Since I figure we're only an hour or two from a hospital, let's get you and your masterpiece cleaned and ready for travel, then let a doctor cut the cord and figure out what else is going on. Sound like a plan?"

Maisey nodded. Exhaustion made her limbs heavy and sluggish. All she wanted to do was hold her baby and sleep.

While Nash tenderly washed her and the baby with warm water, Maisey drifted in and out of consciousness. The baby fed for the first time, and the sensation swelled a whole new range of emotions. She wasn't sure whether she was happy or sad or somewhere in between. In a perfect world, her son's birth should have been a time of elation. But with his father trying to kill her, and take him from her, she couldn't help but feel all the more on edge.

Though the day was sunny and warm, she also couldn't stop shivering.

With Maisey holding the baby, Nash carried her to the truck. He draped Mildred's comforter over the pair, and then climbed behind the wheel.

Had he doused the fire? She lacked the strength to ask—or do much of anything. Her thoughts had turned disjointed and when Nash shut the passenger-side truck door, she rested her head against the cool glass.

Maisey? Mais? Was Nash shaking her? She thought so, but couldn't be sure.

The baby was crying. Maisey needed to get to him, but her arms and legs refused to work.

Mais! Talk to me. What's wrong?

Behind her closed eyes, the day's sun morphed to a chaotic swirl of orange and yellow, and then black . . .

19

Nash drove like the proverbial bat out of hell until thirty minutes later reaching a town. He followed blue hospital signs, and then careened the truck beneath the ER canopy.

A guy in scrubs said, "Sir, you can't park there."

"My wi—" It had been on the tip of Nash's tongue to call Maisey his wife, but she wasn't. To call her his girlfriend felt somehow trite, yet if he were honest with himself, she sure as hell meant more to him than a casual friend. "She had a baby and she's lost a lot of blood."

The baby had been fitfully crying, but was now silent. Nash was in terror that something was wrong with him, too.

The orderly had been on the wrong side of the

truck to have seen Maisey, but he now surged into action. Seconds later, Maisey and her baby had been moved from the truck to a gurney, then whisked behind glass doors.

Nash parked, then hiked back to the bustling ER lobby, unsure what to do with his hands. Yet again, he found himself in the uncomfortable, untenable position of not being in control, and he hated it.

"Sir," a woman asked from behind a reception desk. "Was that your wife you brought in?"

No. But his twisted heart said, "Yes."

"I'll need you to fill out insurance information, then I'll have someone take you to obstetrics to see her."

He nodded, though his brain couldn't quite process what she was saying.

Insurance? He clamped his hand to his forehead. He hadn't even thought about it.

"Sir? If you'll give me your ID and insurance card, I'll get your wife—"

"We don't have insurance."

She raised her eyebrows, looking at him as if sprouts grew from his ears. "You're sure?"

He nodded, then handed her a credit card.

What minimal part of his brain still functioning told Nash that even if he had lots of tidy documentation for Maisey, the last place he could use any of it was here. If Vicente had gone to the trouble to solicit help from his neighbors in finding Maisey, it wasn't a great stretch to assume he probably had a guy in every ER within a couple hundred miles.

After running Nash's card, the clerk asked an ungodly amount of questions that he answered with lies. She next presented him with a stack of papers to sign, which he did. And then a perky volunteer teen dressed in pink scrubs and a bouncy ponytail jabbered a mile a minute about how excited he must be to have a baby while leading him through a maze of corridors.

Nash tried his damnedest to memorize turns, but after about ten, gave up.

All he could think about was how gutted he'd feel if Maisey didn't make it.

He'd already lost one woman he'd loved, because he hadn't been with her. To now lose another? It was unthinkable.

The teen led Nash to a crowded waiting room, handed him a beeper, and told him someone would contact him soon.

Nash stumbled into a dark corner's chair.

A couple of kids stared. Their mom took one startled glance at him, then barked at her rugrats to stay close.

He caught his reflection in the glass of a framed print, and saw why the woman had been alarmed. He looked like a serial killer. As if it wasn't bad enough that he was covered in blood, his clothes were muddy and torn. His face and bare forearms were scratched and bruised and covered in bites.

His chest tightened to think poor Maisey looked even worse.

Pocketing the beeper, he headed for the nearest restroom to at least wash his hands and face. Finished, he looked a little more presentable, but not by much.

What was taking so long? Why hadn't someone let him know the status of Maisey and her baby?

He paced the hall for a good ten minutes, then couldn't tolerate the inaction a moment longer.

A nurse passed with a meds cart.

"Excuse me, ma'am . . ." Nash forced a deep breath and wielded the smile Maisey used to tease would charm the scales off a snake. "My wife and son were taken back a while ago, and I haven't heard any news. Could you please check for me?"

"What's the patient's name?"

"Maisey Adamson." The lie of her being his wife rolled easier and easier off his tongue. She typed the information into a laptop mounted to her cart. "She's in surgery. But your son—"

"Surgery?"

"She'll be fine." She pressed her hand to his upper arm. "In layman's terms, looks like she had a procedure for an invasive placenta. As soon as she's done, your wife's surgeon will be out to tell you more. In the meantime," she pointed toward the nursery. "Your son is doing great. Would you like to hold him?"

"Thanks." Nash had a tough time forcing the lone word through his tight throat.

"Your wife's been assigned to Room 302. Meet me there and I'll bring your son to you."

Tears welling, Nash nodded, then headed that way.

In the minutes before the nurse returned, he paced like a madman.

He needed to call Maisey's mom. She had to be out of her mind with worry. But so was he. Not only was he freaked out about Maisey's well-being, but the fact that at any moment, Vicente and his men could show. Save for a couple knives, Nash was unarmed. Sure, Vicente would have to be an idiot to launch a firefight in a hospital maternity ward, but then Nash had also never expected him to enlist helpers like Harvey and Mildred. He wanted his son, and had already proven he'd go to any lengths to make that acquisition a reality.

Nash thought he could handle this mission solo, but he'd been wrong on that fact, too. Time to call in the cavalry. He'd get Harding and Jasper on the horn, and see which guys were available on short notice.

What they'd do then, he wasn't sure, but preserving his pride was no longer an option. And if he were dead honest with himself, that's what turned this whole thing bad. Having lost Hope while he'd been overseas, he'd told himself that if only he'd been there, maybe she and their baby might have been saved. But clearly he wasn't a one-man solution to Maisey's every problem.

He'd been a damned fool for initially believing he was.

The door opened, and the nurse who had earlier helped, wheeled in a cart that held a clear acrylic tub with Maisey's son. "Here he is." She held out a blue hospital gown. "If you don't mind, since you're a little . . ." She gestured to Nash's muddy, bloody shirt. "Please put this on over your clothes, then wash your hands. Once you're done, have a seat and I'll hand him to you."

"Sure." He took the gown from her, then peered at the baby boy he'd helped bring into the world. "He's so small."

"Five pounds, twelve-ounces. I've seen bigger, but his lungs are strong, and he has a great appetite. As soon as Mommy's feeling better, she can start breastfeeding."

"Good." After completing his assigned lists of prerequisites for holding the infant, he sat on the upholstered bench seat that ran the length of the room's large picture window.

"One more thing." She took a hospital name band from the pocket of her scrub top. "If you could please show me ID, you'll need to wear this as long as your little one is admitted. It's a safety precaution." She smiled. "We haven't switched a baby yet, but these days, you never can be too careful."

"True." He showed her his driver's license, washed his hands again, settled back onto his former bench seat, then held out his arms to receive precious cargo.

"Here you go. Have you and your wife decided on a name?"

"No." The pink-cheeked, blanket-wrapped bundle looked nothing like the infant Nash had in a small way helped bring into the world. His throat ached with awe, fear for what nasty surprises Vicente might next pull, and determination to keep this precious being safe—no matter the personal cost.

Staring into the tiny creature's blue eyes, Nash felt lost, but then found. The infant was a miracle in every sense of the word, and his mother deserved all the credit.

The nurse said, "Press the call button if you two need anything."

"Thanks. I will." Nash had been so absorbed in thoughts of this little guy's future that he'd forgotten she was in the room.

"Hey," he said to him once she'd gone. "You look a lot more handsome after a proper bath." Careful to keep his touch feather light, Nash traced his fingertip along the infant's faint brows. "Your mommy should be coming back to us soon. Are you as excited to see her as I am?"

Of course, the little guy didn't answer, but Nash's aching heart did.

His instant connection with her son proved he still cared for Maisey—had always cared for her—which made him feel all the more traitorous to the memory of his wife. In the same breath, he couldn't wait for Maisey to return. Not just to this room, but to him. *Us.* How had all the emotion he'd once felt for her come rushing back so fast? Where had all of that been? Or had he been fooling himself all those years, to think it had ever been fully gone?

The door creaked open. Elated that Maisey had returned, Nash looked up, only he didn't find the woman to whom he had so much to say, but a man in a dark suit and mirrored sunglasses.

Vicente?

Pulse surging, Nash tightened his hold on Maisey's son.

20

Maisey was slow to wake.

Her memories of her son's birth and what happened after were at best, vague. Nothing more than flashes of dappled sunshine skipping atop her closed eyes as Nash carried her and her son to their borrowed truck. And then the cool glare of fluorescents when strangers explained she'd lost a lot of blood and needed surgery.

Now, her mouth and throat tasted like she'd downed cotton balls for dinner, followed by thumbtacks for dessert.

On the bright side, she was excited to see her baby. And Nash. He'd saved her life yet again, and she couldn't wait to thank him.

Where was he?

She fully opened her eyes for her first look at her latest surroundings. Heat and bugs and impenetrable green had been replaced by soothing pale blue walls, striped curtains, a dim light glowing above a counter sink, and a dark window looking out upon a twinkling nighttime view. She didn't have a clue what city she was in, let alone the name of the hospital. All she did know was that thanks to Nash, she and her baby were finally safe.

She happily stretched, breathing deeply of the cool air. Despite the faint antiseptic smell, she had no complaints. In fact, after the past couple days, she was pretty sure she'd never complain again.

A knock on the door startled her, but then, expecting Nash—maybe even her mother, if he'd been thoughtful enough to call—she smiled at his dark figure. "Hey. This is sure an upgrade from our last hangout."

He stepped into the faint light, and she froze.

The man wasn't Nash, but a hulking stranger. One of Vicente's men?

"Nurse!" Pulse racing, she fumbled for the nurse's call button.

"Relax . . ." He held out his hands palms up. "My name is Harding Breslow. Nash and I go way back. I'm here to help."

"Help with what?" Her gaze darted about the room, searching for a weapon or an escape route. She had to find her baby and Nash. No way would he have left her alone.

"You've been out of it for a while, and there's no easy way to say this, so I'm going to come right out with it. Your ex stopped by for a visit. He—"

"Wait. What?" Barely able to hear her voice above her pounding heart, Maisey needed time to process the man's words. "Where's my son? And Nash? Are they hurt?"

He winced. "For now, I'm assuming they're safe. Ten hours ago, I was in my Denver office when Nash called me collect. We only spoke for a few minutes before he was cut off, and I hopped a charter flight. All I caught was that he has your baby, and that he's headed for where you had your *first time*. Does that make sense?"

The Holiday Inn. But it was hours from here. Nash wouldn't have left her unless . . . The thought of Vicente having been here, in this very room, made her skin crawl. She pressed harder on the nurse's call button.

"Yes?" a muffled voice asked over the intercom.
"Help!" Maisey cried. "I need help!"

Her door burst open, and a nurse followed by a uniformed cop and a guy in a rumpled suit burst through.

Eyes tearing, heart hammering at a frightening pace, Maisey clutched her sheets to her chest. "I don't know this man, and he said someone took my baby?"

The man who claimed to be Nash's friend retreated to the room's shadows. "Ma'am," the man in the suit stepped forward. "I'm Detective Howard with the Stanhope Police Department. I realize you are understandably upset, but here are the facts as we know them. At seven thirty-five yesterday evening, a nurse entered your room to check on your husband and baby. When she returned approximately thirty minutes later to find them both gone, she alerted hospital security, who alerted local authorities of a suspected kidnapping. Hospital security footage shows a man holding your husband at gunpoint while leading him out of the facility. Once outside, your husband kicked the gun from the assailant, then fled. The assailant was rendered unconscious, but upon waking, also fled in a black SUV. We were unable to get a positive ID on the license. Here's the tricky part. This man claiming to be your husband, isn't really your husband at all, is he? We did some rudimentary background checks, and turns out you're actually married to Vicente Rodriguez who is claiming custody of your child. He's paid your bill in full, and has hired a team of attorneys to secure custody of his son. The man who has your child—the man claiming to be your husband? He's been charged with kidnapping." *Nash was now in trouble?*

"That's crazy. I can explain. My true husband is a monster—we're not really even married." *Would this nightmare ever end?* Maisey tugged at the needle

146

taped to the top of her left hand. "If you'd help me get this IV out, I'll take you to him."

"Not so fast," the detective said while writing notes in a pocket-sized spiral notebook. "We see this sort of thing more often than you'd think. Who you choose to have relations with is your thing, but if your son has Vicente Rodriguez's DNA, then he needs to be returned to his father. End of story. If you know where the man posing as your husband might be, you need to tell us now, before criminal charges are also filed against you."

"No. You have it all wrong. I can explain." She forced a deep breath, then admitted, "Vicente Rodriguez is my son's true biological father. I can only assume my friend, Nash, lied to hospital admissions to protect my identity in case my ex pulled a stunt like this."

By the time the detective finished questioning her at length about the crimes she'd witnessed Vicente and his men commit, dawn streaked the horizon in bands of yellow and gold. The only thing keeping Maisey from losing control was the knowledge that as long as her baby was with Nash, he would be safe—not that the fact made her anymore happy about her temporary separation from either of them, but as soon as she ditched her entourage, they'd soon be reunited.

"Harding?" She yawned from exhaustion, but until she found her son, there was no way she'd find sleep.

"Yes, ma'am." He answered with a thick Southern drawl.

"Will you take me to my baby and Nash?"

"That's the plan. He texted me an hour ago from a burner phone. But don't you have recovering to do?"

She shook her head. "I'll rest on the way."

"I don't know . . ." He gestured toward her IV and row of monitors. "Sure you're feeling up to this? You had a baby, then surgery."

"Ever heard the expression not to mess with a momma bear?"

"Say no more." He reached into the backpack he'd held beside him on the bench window seat. "While you were with the detective, I found these for you in the gift shop." He set a predominantly pink wad of clothes topped by pink flip-flops on the foot of the bed. "Guessed on the size."

"Thanks. Really."

He flashed a tight smile. "I've had triage medical training. Let me help with your IV."

Maisey closed her eyes while he took her hand, withdrawing the business-end of her tubing. It stung, but only for a moment after he'd added a cotton ball and then medical tape. The pang of missing her son and Nash hurt far worse.

Once freed, she made a solo trek to the restroom. Dressing was no easy feat, yet determination proved more valuable than strength in tossing off her hospital-issued blue gown, then stepping into the shower. She would have skipped it to save time, but one look in the mirror told her there was no way she'd ever pass for normal without basic personal hygiene.

Freshly scrubbed, she towel-dried, then tugged on elastic-waisted pink capris and a matching cotton T-shirt bearing a pink-sequined flamingo. Not exactly subtle, but it was clean and would be cool in the summer heat. She slipped her feet into the flip-flops, skimmed her damp curls into a neat ponytail, then forced a deep breath.

You can do this, she coached the shell-shocked stranger in the mirror.

She forced down the knot of fear lodged at the back of her throat, then left the bathroom to tell Harding she was ready.

On the walk from her room to the elevators, Maisey's heart beat so loud she feared passing staff members might hear. But they hadn't, and so she focused on each step, forcing her wobbly legs to move.

Harding was kind, offering his arm for her to hold for support.

"How do you know Nash?" she asked during the short journey down.

"We met during our SEAL training, then got as-signed to the same team. We were the only two

Southern gentlemen, meaning the guys gave us more than our fair share of grief."

A soft ding alerted them that the elevator had reached the lobby-level.

Harding guided her through a maze of people to the hospital's entry. "Smile and try to act normal. Pretty sure we're being followed, but I'll ditch them as soon as we hit traffic."

While struggling for her next panicked breath, she forced her lips to curve upward. Would Vicente never quit?

"Do you feel strong enough to walk to my ride?"

"Yes. I think so." Her rubbery legs weren't so sure. With every step, muggy, early morning air took superhuman effort to drag in. Heat already rose from the blacktop, and she was creeped out by the almost certain fact that somewhere amongst this sea of cars, Vicente or his men watched.

"Good. It's a bad idea for us to separate, or for me to carry you—I don't want to draw attention—but I could snag a wheelchair if you—"

"I'm fine," she snapped. "Please get me to Nash and my son."

"Yes, ma'am."

He led her to a black Hummer.

Before she had a chance to ponder how she'd climb in, he settled his hands around her waist, giving her a chaste boost into the passenger seat.

She thanked him, but her words were lost when he left her to walk around the car and get settled behind the wheel.

With the engine started, he zigzagged through the lot, checking the rearview with every turn for *company*. "Depending on traffic, our trip's going to take about five hours. You'd make me feel better about springing you from the hospital if you'd get some rest."

"I will, but not until we're on the interstate."

"Fair enough."

They made it to I-95 without incident. Maisey wished she could stay awake, but her body had a different plan. She woke hours later, not sure whether her breasts, abdomen, or heart hurt most. She opened her eyes to catch slivers of urban sprawl passing by.

"Where are we?" she asked.

"About thirty minutes south of Jacksonville proper."

"Great." she managed a faint smile. "But first, would you mind stopping at a convenience store? I could use a restroom."

"You got it."

She sipped from a bottled water, but managed to spill more down her sequined flamingo than she drank.

"There should be napkins in the glove box," Harding pointed that direction.

"Thanks." She opened the compartment and grabbed a few. She was on the verge of closing it when a pamphlet caught her eye. It was a promotional piece for one of Vicente's pet charities. *The Little House that Love Built* was an Orlando-based foundation for pediatric cancer victims. It paid their expenses, and sent them to theme parks. It made Vicente look like a saint instead of the monster he was. The fact that Harding had the pamphlet raised red flags. She took it out, and flashed it to him. "What are you doing with this?"

"Research."

She returned it to the glove box and shut the door. His answer was plausible, but what if like Mildred and Harvey he'd been bought? Just how well did Nash know him?

Her pulse raged with fresh fear. What should she do?

He took the next exit, and a few minutes later, eased the massive vehicle alongside the convenience store's north side, aiming it outward, she assumed for ease if they needed to make a quick getaway.

She yawned. "On second thought, I don't need the restroom, but I'm awfully thirsty and spilled the last of my water." She rubbed her throat. "Think the thirst is a side-effect from surgery?"

He eyed her funny, then killed the engine. "I'll help you inside."

"If you don't mind, I'd rather stay in the car. I

don't have the energy to budge. Could you pretty please grab me a Sprite? Oh—and if you don't mind, could you leave the motor running. It's already too hot to be trapped in here with no air."

"You're not thinking of pulling a fast one on me, are you?" His eyes narrowed. "This Vicente character is freakishly well-connected. He has eyes everywhere."

"Where would I go?" she asked with what she hoped came across as an innocent tone. Better than anyone, she realized how dangerous the man she'd believed to be her husband truly was. That's why she needed to escape Harding. Sure, he said he knew Nash, but what proof did she really have? What if he'd had the brochure for personal reasons? Maybe he had a child—a niece or nephew—with cancer, and Vicente offered to fund their cure? With Nash and her baby's lives at stake, she could never be too careful.

"Exactly." He roared the engine back to life, then cranked the air to high. "Hungry? Want me to grab you a pudding or crackers?"

"Both, please. You're a doll."

He winced. "I've been called a lot of things in my years, but never that. Be right back."

"Thanks." Big smile.

She waited until he vanished amongst the lunch crowd rush to gingerly ease behind the driver's seat and gun the engine forward. In panic mode, she killed it, and then couldn't get it started. Her heart hammered to the point of pain. She was out of breath and frenzied, but forced a deep inhalation and tried again while Harding tore out of the store's double doors.

She pressed the driver's side auto-lock button.

"Don't do this!" he shouted. "You're being a fool!"

"How do I know Vicente hasn't bribed you? I have to get to Nash—warn him that you're crooked!" With her line of sight narrowed to a slim black-ringed tunnel, she scooted to the seat's edge to gain better control of the gas pedal. The vehicle was enormous, and to stand a better chance of escape, she eased out of the lot, uncaring that Harding ran alongside her.

"Pull over!" he shouted. "I told you, the stupid pamphlet was research!"

"I don't trust you!" She'd convinced Nash to drop his guard around Mildred and Harvey, and look what a disaster that turned out to be. She refused to take one more unnecessary risk. Even though Harding knew where she was headed, she'd hopefully beat him by enough time for her and Nash and the baby to run.

Biting her lower lip, gripping the wheel tight enough to hurt, she merged left, only daring to breathe once she'd made it a few miles down I-95.

I did it.

Elation was short-lived when she fumbled for the power button to ease her seat further forward, but at least she was on the right track. She hadn't been anywhere near the Holiday Inn where she and Nash had spent the night of their first prom in over a decade, but that was okay. Some things you never forget, and that night was certainly one of them.

The hotel was near the airport, so she followed the signs.

Fifteen minutes later, after a wrong turn on a one-way highway access road, she careened the vehicle into the hotel lot. She parked it in the rear, backing it in with the use of a rear-mounted camera.

Physical pain threatened to shut her down, but she refused to let it. As soon as she and Nash and her baby were safe, she'd take time to properly heal. Until then, she fought for even shallow breaths.

Outside the car's cool temperature, hot, humid air raised goose bumps on her forearms.

The jolt on her abdomen and spine from the hop from the driver's seat to the blacktop proved agonizing. She froze a moment to regain her composure, then aimed for the hotel's rear door, praying at this time of day it would be unlocked.

It was, and not wanting to risk possible exposure by wandering around, looking for an elevator, she ducked through a door promising stairwell access.

Room 777.

Please, let Nash and my baby be there.

Trembling from exhaustion brought on by the punishment her body had been through, she gripped the rail. The first flight was torture. The second flight—hell. By the time she'd finished the third, the walls blurred and her every breath became a struggle.

For an instant, she squeezed her eyes shut and focused on her baby. Nash.

She reminded herself how literally her entire life depended on getting the rest of the way up these stairs. Over and over she repeated the climbing motion until finally spotting the *Seventh Floor* sign.

She dragged the heavy fire door open, pulling herself through.

Wobbling like a drunk, she zigzagged the endless corridor until finally spotting their room—*lucky 777.*

Dizzy with relief, she pounded the heels of her fists against the door. "Nash! Nash, it's me. Let me in. Harding's not who you think!"

He opened the door, only when she glanced up to lose herself in the sight of his dear features, she realized she'd made a horrible mistake.

The stranger gazing back at her wasn't Nash . . .

21

"Maisey? Can you hear me?" Nash's chest walls could hardly contain his heart's frantic beats. After all they'd been through, if she died . . . He refused to finish the thought—not because he would allow himself to need her in his life, but because the more he was around her, the more he realized his feelings went so much deeper than friendship.

He didn't know what that meant, and sure as hell didn't have time to dissect the meaning of the knot lodged at the back of his throat or the tears stinging his eyes. All he knew with one hundred percent certainty was that if the worst were to happen, he wasn't sure how he'd go on. "Angel, you're safe, and so is your son. I've got him right here. I know you're tired, but open your eyes at least long enough to let me know you're okay."

With the help of his friend and associate, Jasper, Nash carried Maisey's limp form to the room's bed. She'd collapsed at the door—no doubt exhausted from fleeing the hospital and then Harding.

Nash's boss was understandably pissed about having his pride and joy custom Hummer hijacked— Harding had flown to Miami from Denver, but had Jasper drive the vehicle carrying their firepower. He understood Maisey's reasoning, and Nash had already sent their pal, Briggs, to retrieve him.

Nash perched on the edge of the bed. "Come on, Mais. Wake up."

What was in reality only a minute seemed to take lifetimes. Her breathing was shallow, and her coloring *off*. Harding had a network of discreet doctors on call for the firm, and he'd promised one was already on the way.

"*Please*, angel." *Come back to me*. Nash had nothing to offer her by way of the sort of permanent commitment she deserved. He had no house, and half the time, his battered truck that was still down in the Everglades refused to run. He hadn't even worked out what remained of his feelings for Hope, but he was trying. One thing he had learned was that he no longer wanted to be alone. More specifically, he no longer wanted to be without Maisey—the girl, now woman, who'd been first in his heart, and who he now recognized had never left his soul. "Please . . ."

Her eyelids fluttered. "Nash?"

"I'm right here." His breath caught in his throat.

"My baby?"

"He's here, too." While blinking his stinging eyes in relief, he held up her swaddled son. "We've been bonding over room service and ESPN."

"Look at you," she whispered to her newborn. Her eyes welled with tears. "You're beautiful."

Not half as good looking as his momma.

"There were so many stairs . . . When the door opened, and you weren't here . . ."

"Sorry I gave you a scare. While I was on diaper duty, Jasper manned the door."

"Hey." His friend waved from the foot of the bed. "Sorry we didn't meet under better circumstances."

Maisey managed a faint smile, then drifted back to sleep.

The doctor came and went, explaining that her vitals were good, but she needed rest. Lots.

Briggs returned with Harding, and now the four of them sat around the adjoining room's coffee table, munching burgers and tossing around ideas for catching Vicente. Harding's police contacts had said the compound where Maisey had been held was empty, as was a Miami residence owned under the corporate umbrella of Rodriguez, Intl.

The man had for all practical purposes evaporated, which did little to ease Nash's worry.

"The way I see it," Nash said. "We've got two options. Either flush him out by planting a story in the media or hunt him like the dog he is."

"Personally," Jasper dredged a fry in ketchup. "I enjoy the hell out of a good hunt. Woof-woof, motherfucker."

"Ditto." Briggs stole one of Jasper's fries. At five-eleven, Briggs was the smallest on their team, but the guy ate more than all of them put together.

"Look," Nash said, "no one would rather eradicate that sonofabitch in a seriously painful, creative way more than me, but the bottom line is Maisey and the baby's well-being. My FBI contact says the feds have been tracking this guy for years, waiting for him to slip up. Even if he surfaces, they have nothing but hearsay to charge him with. With Maisey, they'll at least have an eyewitness to murder, drug trafficking, kidnapping, etc. I say flush him, then let him fend for himself. Though I'm not sure how Maisey feels."

"There are merits to both directions." Harding finished off his burger. "But I agree, the most—"

"Kill him . . ." Maisey emerged from the adjoining room. She held her son in her arms, and though an air of exhaustion still clung to deep shadows beneath her eyes, her coloring had improved and her gaze shone with steel. "He's a monster."

"There you have it," Jasper said. "A woman after my own heart."

Clinging to the door jamb for support, she said, "When I think of all he put me through—indirectly, his own son—it makes me sick. Then, there's this kidnapping charge against Nash. We could spend years watching our backs while he dances around the legal systems with high-priced lawyers, I can't . . ." She bowed her head. "I can't imagine living scared one more day. Harding—I'm so sorry for taking off without you. See? That's how crazy this man makes me."

"We're good," Harding assured. "I like your spunk."

Nash went to her, slipping his arm around her fragile form. In such a short time, she'd come to mean the world to him all over again. She'd become that much more precious as a package deal with her son. He wasn't saying he was ready to leap back into anything official, but he wanted to, and that was confusing as hell.

"Here's what I think we should do." Nash tucked one of Maisey's flyaway curls behind her ear. "This isn't the Wild West, so as much as I'd enjoy shooting Vicente between his black eyes, I legally don't have that luxury. Harding," he looked to the hulking form who'd pilfered a trio of Briggs' fries, "do you still have that bigwig press contact in DC?"

"Sure, but how's that going to help us flush a

guy in Florida?"

"It won't unless you manage to wrangle us a mighty big favor. Here's what I'll need you to do . . ."

22

Thursday morning, two days after her hospital escape, Maisey felt infinitely stronger and more like herself.

Nash had moved her from the hotel to a safe house, and had even brought both of their mothers along for the ride. He'd told her they were there to help with the baby and keep her company, but she knew better. He was afraid Vicente might use one of them as a bargaining chip to get his hands on her son. She loved Nash all the more for ensuring that wouldn't happen.

While he and Harding and more of the men he worked with put their complex plan to catch Vicente into motion, she waited. And wrung her hands and wished and prayed for the whole mess to soon be over.

That afternoon, after putting her son down for a nap, she joined her mother, Maxine, and Nash's mom, Gloria, on the screened porch surrounding an elaborate free-form pool and waterfall. The two women played mahjong as if neither had a care in the world and viewed this intrusion upon their lives as a vacation. Maxine had aged well, and rocked faded jeans and a Krispy Kreme Donuts T-shirt she'd won at Bingo. She wore her dyed strawberry blond hair in a sassy short cut, and never left her bedroom in the morning without full make-up. Gloria was a retired nurse, but still wore colorful scrubs with sneakers. Today's selection were baby blue, dotted with pacifiers and rattles—in honor of Maisey's son. She also wore her hair short, but it had turned gray. She'd never had the time nor the patience for make-up.

The two women had been friends and neighbors for as long as Maisey could remember. That lifelong bond was comforting—to a point. As much as Maisey enjoyed having her two moms with her, she was now as scared for them as she was for herself, her son, and Nash.

The six-bedroom home was located in an affluent Jacksonville suburb, and Nash had left all of them in the capable hands of four stone-faced men who weren't especially chatty, but seemed intent on doing their job. Nash explained that the place belonged to a businessman they'd helped out of a dicey situation. He was currently working in China and welcomed them to stay indefinitely. All of which was convenient, but hardly put Maisey at ease. The thought that somewhere out there, Vicente was stalking her to get his hands on their son made bile rise in her throat.

"Why so glum?" Gloria asked after placing her latest tile.

"I'm restless. Nash should have called by now."

"Relax," Maxine took her turn. "You and the baby are safe and well protected. You'll hear from him soon."

"You know what I want to hear about . . ." Gloria shared a laugh with Maxine, then they toasted with their lemonades. "During all that time you and Nash were on the run, were there sparks?"

I wish. "You mean other than the ones coming from gun barrels?"

Maxine cringed.

Gloria shuddered. "I'll never get used to my son being in danger. He was upset about leaving the Navy, but I was secretly relieved. Then he joined this security firm and he's right back in perpetual trouble. I'd hoped he'd settle down to a nice job in sales."

"You know that sort of thing isn't in his nature," Maxine pointed out. "Even as a little boy, he was chasing around the neighborhood, saving little kids from bullies and Maisey from that blasted treehouse the two of them built. I lost count of how many times you got yourself trapped up there by knocking down the ladder."

"To be fair," Maisey found a faint smile, "it happened plenty of times to Nash, too . . ."

"True," Gloria said with a wistful expression. "Life was simpler when getting stuck in a tree was the extent of my worries about him. When he was deployed, I was lucky to get a couple hours of sleep each night. And then when his sweet wife was the one who ended up dying in that fire . . ." She shook her head. "It was beyond tragic. They'd tried years to get pregnant. Nash was beyond inconsolable. I'd thought I'd lost him to a place darker than death. But then you went and got yourself in trouble again, and in saving you, he seems to have a found a new lease on life."

"*Gee*, glad I could help," Maisey said with a wry smile.

"You never seriously answered my question." Gloria took a sugar cookie from a plate in the center of the table. "Do you think there's a chance for you and my son to once again be an item?"

"No," Maisey said with a firm shake of her head. Not because she didn't want that, but because Nash had admitted he wasn't ready. Might never be. The fact broke her heart all over again, but considering she'd been the one who'd initially rejected him, then gotten herself messed up with a drug dealing psychopath, she couldn't exactly blame Nash for shying away.

Incapable of answering more questions and desperately needing space, she wandered through the sprawling home to her bedroom, where her son slept peacefully in the portable crib one of Nash's coworkers had delivered. There was also a stroller and changing table and mounds of clothes, diapers, bottles and formula. Her son still didn't have a name, which greatly bothered her, but the stress of escaping Vicente, and then that detective's ugly accusations at the hospital had her all messed up. Naming her son implied a future she was terrified they might not share. But if that were the case, then she should name him—now—to banish the dark fear clawing her mind.

Craving fresh air, she went to her room's balcony, and stood at the wrought iron rail, staring at the golf course and the swampy marsh beyond. She dragged in the moist, briny air praying for clarity and safety and peace. Most of all, she prayed for Nash's safe return. And for him to tell her Vicente was gone, that there'd been no more violence, and he'd conveniently vanished, guaranteed never to return again. But that was a fairy tale.

A golfer hit his ball into the house's backyard.

He drove his cart to retrieve it, caught sight of her and waved.

She waved back, glad to feel somewhat normal

for at least a few seconds.

But then one of the security goons stepped around from the side of the house, and asked the man to move along. The golfer retreated, reminding Maisey that far from what her mother chose to believe, this place was no vacation home, but instead another gilded cage she'd been forced into to save herself and her son from the man she'd once loved.

Back in her room, she perched on the edge of her bed, staring at her sleeping child. "Why can't I name you?" she whispered. "How can I love you with every breath of my being, but be terrified you're only a dream?"

A knock sounded on her bedroom door, startling her and making her feel silly for asking such deep questions of an only days-old infant.

"There you are." When Nash entered, a rush of elation swelled, only to fade when he didn't smile or step closer for a hug, or do any of the myriad of things a man who'd missed a woman might do. "This house is a trip, huh?"

"It's huge, but Vicente has half a dozen even larger."

"Swell . . ."

"Did you find him?" she was almost afraid to ask.

He winced. "Not exactly."

Her stomach churned. "What's that mean?"

"We've got trouble." He took a folded newspaper clipping from a side pocket of his black cargo pants, spread it open, then set it on the bed. It was the front page of the Miami Herald and read: *Philanthropist Offers Five Million for Safe Return of Kidnapped Wife and Infant Son.* Alongside the article were full-color photos of not only herself, but Nash as well. "This ran in nearly every newspaper in Florida and neighboring states. Even worse—he's being interviewed on local and national news. With that much money at stake, people are hunting you for cash and me for sport. Since I was the one seen on hospital security with your son . . ." He shrugged.

"What about what I told police? That Vicente's the true criminal. Why haven't they taken him into custody? This makes no sense."

"Welcome to the American justice system. At this point, it's your word against his, and apparently his lawyers win at working the media machine."

"I thought you and Harding were working your own media angle? You promised this would be over soon." Her throat ached with frustrated tears, but she had none left.

"It will . . ." He stepped toward her, wrapping his arms around her, but she lurched free.

"No, Nash. It won't. Not ever. Guys like him always win, and the stupid, moonstruck girls who think he's their savior lose. Worst part is that there's no one but myself to blame. But I can fix it. By God, for the sake of my son, I will force police to realize Vicente is to blame for all of this—certainly not you." She marched to her balcony door and thrust it open. Outside, she shouted to everyone on the crowded golf course, "Hey! Look at me! This is what five million—"

"What's wrong with you?" Nash grabbed her from behind, clamping his hand over her mouth. "Have you got some kind of death wish?"

She put up a strong fight to break free, but it was no use. In her weakened condition she was outmatched. Once Nash had her safely back inside with the curtains drawn, he released her.

"Don't do that again. We can protect you against one man, but now that Vicente's employed practically the whole, damned state, we've got to be all the more careful."

"What good will that do? Other than prolonging the inevitable?"

"It will keep you and your baby safe." This time when he pulled her into his arms, she let him. Those brief shining moments of absolute security served as a godsend, bolstering her strength and resolve to see this through. "From where I'm standing, that's a very good thing."

"Why do you even care? It's not like you want me." She hated her petulant tone, but her statement was true. Even if by some miracle they managed to escape her ex, then what? Would Nash go on to his next mission and leave her to begin the rest of her life as a single mom? She was beyond excited about raising her son—whatever the circumstances. But it would certainly be more fun with the man she loved—had always loved—alongside her.

"That's BS, and you know it." Gripping her shoulders, he eased her back, staring into her eyes with enough intensity to make her shiver. Their mouths were close enough for her to feel his warm exhalations. The familiar scent of his breath made her punch drunk-dizzy with irrational longings. "You and me—it's no secret we share incredible history, but until this mess with Vicente is cleared up, my role is to protect you—not kiss you. Besides, you know I owe it to my wife to remain faithful."

"Your dead wife?" Screw it. Maisey once again wrestled away, but he was pulling her back. "I'm such a fool. This whole situation has me losing my mind."

"Then we're even." He was beside her again, resting his forehead against hers.

Despite a distinct lack of exertion, both breathed heavy.

"Thinking of you and the baby makes me crazy," he said. "I can't stop wondering how great it would be to buy a house near our moms and make a family—just like we always wanted. But I can't erase the fact that I already had a wife, and I almost had a son. They can't be replaced like old car batteries. They were alive and a few days earlier I'd heard our baby's heartbeat via Skype, and then both of them were gone. I can't forget, Mais. I owe it to them to never forget."

"I-I understand." But she didn't. Not really. Of course, she grasped his need to continue loving those he'd lost. But she was right here, standing before him, heart beating strong and true. She wanted to be the one who comforted him and reassured him that he had permission to resume his life. Sadly, she lacked the power. And since she had been the one who'd pushed him away all those years ago, she also lacked the right.

Her baby released a few fitful cries. She went to him, glad for something to do other than think about how different her life might now be had she married Nash when he'd asked.

"All right, well . . ." Nash crossed his arms. "I'll leave you to it."

Without a sound, she watched him go.

"Sweetie," she whispered to her son on her way to a rocking chair to feed him. "How is it that the whole time we were stuck in that smelly swamp, Nash and I connected like we used to, yet now, we feel like strangers?"

Of course, her wide-eyed son had no more answers than she did.

"I need to name you." While he fed from her breast, she traced the tip of her pinkie down his cheek. "And then I need to get back to reality. I used to be lucky enough to work with my best friend, but things between us went sour." She smoothed the crown of her baby's head. "Delia and I used to own the sweetest dress shop. We sold pretty purses and evening gowns and shoes, but your mommy went and did something not so smart when she let Vicente talk her into selling her half." She refused to call that monster her son's father. A man had to earn that title. "Because I love you, maybe I'll start a new business. When you're older, you can help. We'll be a team. Together, we'll be a spectacular duo."

Her words sounded more reassuring than they felt.

Still, she was determined to make at least one part of her life right, so when her son finished snacking, she climbed onto the king-sized bed, tucked him alongside her, then used the house's landline to call the Centre Street boutique, *Glad Rags*, she used to spend so much time at that she considered it home.

"It's a great day to look your best. This is Delia. May I help you?"

"Dee, it's Maisey."

"Where are you? You're all over the news. Are you all right? Did Nash really take you against your will? Because back when we were in school, seemed like you were fully consenting."

"Ha ha. I am with Nash, but only because he's trying to help. My mom got him involved, and—"

"Is she with you, too? When I first saw the news story, I called her but got no answer." Maisey was touched that her friend had been concerned for her well-being.

"Yes. She's here, along with Nash's mom. He thought they would both be safer that way."

"This is incredible—like something out of a movie."

"I know, right?" It felt amazing to be chatting with her friend like old times. Normal. And at the moment, that was what she most craved. They hadn't left off on the best of terms. For a while, Maisey had needed to apologize. Finally, now was her chance.

"Listen to me, rambling when you probably had a reason for calling. How can I help?"

Maisey's eyes once again stung. "I wanted to apologize for leaving you in the lurch, but mostly, I wanted to help you. To warn you that you might be in danger."

"You know I can take care of myself." There was a long pause. "As for that apology, it's not necessary. You and I will always be friends."

"Thanks." Now it was Maisey taking time to find her composure. Her friend's kind words meant the world. "But I made a big mistake with this guy. He's dangerous. I don't think he'd come after you to find me, but I can't be sure. Promise you'll at least be careful?"

"Promise. Now, get back to your gorgeous baby and handsome man."

Maisey wished Nash was her man.

After saying their goodbyes, Maisey hung up. She felt wistful for old times when she and Delia and Nash had been like three amigos. With those days long gone, all she could do was focus on her hopefully Vicente-free future. She'd get a small business loan and open her own shop. She could take her son with her to work—maybe even rent a storefront with an efficiency apartment above? Everything would work out fine.

Except for her broken heart . . .

23

Vicente Rodriguez was a ghost.

For all of his previous visibility, intel now showed no satellite photos of movement between his three south Florida homes, and he'd closed all online accounts. Nash hadn't been surprised to find that the Stanhope police force had made a recent purchase of thirty patrol cars—one for each man on the force, plus ten spare. Detective Howard retired and moved to a swanky gated community in Belize. Had that been the going rate for his soul?

Nash had become a fugitive. The media machine pegged him as a violent, mentally-unhinged kidnapper, who was a breath away from stealing newborns and eating them for breakfast.

Meanwhile, the shadows beneath Maisey's eyes

had darkened, and far from her being a content new mom, she was fidgety and gloomy.

Her fitful baby mirrored her mood.

Nash pitched the sub sandwich Jasper had brought him back onto its paper wrap, and shoved it across the outdoor kitchen's counter. It was two in the morning. Almost time for his turn at the nightly watch to end.

Above the pool chemicals' chlorine scent rose dank musk from the nearby marsh. Crickets chirped. The occasional frog croaked and dogs barked, but otherwise, all was quiet in their temporary world.

A liberal dowsing of bug spray even kept mosquitoes at bay.

Nash should have been confident and calm, but the truth was that his stomach sat on a knife's edge, constantly at war with any given meal. He no longer gave a damn about himself, but what was happening with Maisey wasn't right. She deserved to have her life back. She needed the comfort of knowing that if she chose to take her son for a stroll, they'd be safe. She'd grown weary of constantly looking over her shoulder, and he couldn't blame her.

He was tired, too.

At times, he selfishly wished her mother had never gotten him mixed up in Maisey's case. He'd been better off alone, before he'd remembered how good they'd once been.

In the swamp, with her covered in dirt, scratches

and bites, it had been easier to remind himself Maisey was his latest assignment—nothing more. But here, in the kind of mansion he'd once dreamed of providing for her, it grew increasingly harder to maintain a detached professionalism. Each time she swept her long curls up from her neck, he fought not to brush his lips along her elegant throat. She'd long ago harbored fantasies of becoming a ballerina. Back in junior high, he and his mother had gone to one of Maisey's shows. She hadn't been the star, but in his eyes, she might as well have been the only girl onstage. She'd worn glittery pink and looked like the spinning dancer inside of his mother's favorite jewelry box.

Back then, anything had seemed possible.

Now, reality served daily doses of truth. His truth? He'd had his grand shot at love with Hope and lost it. Now, he wasn't even sure what love meant or entailed—certainly far more than he had available to emotionally give.

Jasper wandered up. "Ready for some shut-eye?"

"Nah. I'm all right, if you've got something you'd rather do."

"Cool," he chuckled. "I'll head down to the Bahamas for a while. Catch a few conch, maybe a nice, juicy grouper. I'll cook myself a damned fine meal."

"Sounds like a plan."

"Oh—wait until I tell you about my companion..." He whistled. "She's a looker. Long, dark hair and eyes as green as lime Jell-O."

"Is she an alien?" Nash couldn't resist teasing. "Don't know if I'm into the whole green Jell-O thing?"

"Screw you. You know what I mean. Her name's Eden, and I'm seriously into her—only one problem."

"She's not into ugly guys like you?"

"Ha ha. Point of fact, she's an English lit professor, but her dad studies microbes. She leaves in November for a year in the Antarctic. She plans to use the isolation to write a novel."

"Huh?" Nash scratched his head. "Why the hell would anyone voluntarily go there? More importantly, why would a smarty like her be into a dunce like you?"

"You're quite the jokester tonight.

"I try." Nash grinned. It felt unexpectedly good to crack a smile. For days—hell, months—he'd walked around like the Grim Reaper, mourning the passing of his wife and unborn son. He didn't deserve happiness, and because of that fact, he resumed his usual frown.

"And he's back . . ."

"What are you talking about?"

"Dude, your scowl has become epic. Loosen up. You've got a gal in the house who's crazy about you. Do what you do, then get on with your life."

"What exactly do I do?" From Nash's point of

view, from the start of his marriage and certainly Maisey's rescue, he hadn't tried doing anything hard enough. If he had, he'd still be married today. Maisey would be wholly safe. "From where I'm sitting, it feels like my life has become one, big series of screw-ups."

"Knock it off. Losing Hope and the baby was a tough break, but she could outdrink any of us and had a laugh that transported you to the sun." Eyes shining in the dim light, he placed his hand over his heart. "She was incredible. We all loved her. But she's been gone a while, yet you haven't even kind-of moved on."

"Thanks, Dr. Phil." A muscle ticked in Nash's jaw from pure annoyance.

"All I'm saying is that with Maisey and her baby boy, fate set a perfect do-over in your lap. Don't screw it up."

I already have.

24

"What are you doing?" Nash asked Maisey a little past ten the next morning. He'd finally gotten a few hours' shut-eye and felt only half as morose as he had the night before. Huge improvement, right?

"Finding a place to jump-start my life." She sat at the mansion's glass-top kitchen table, circling newspaper ads. Her baby lounged in his carrier in a sunny patch alongside her chair. "As soon as we're out of here, I'm going to open my own second-hand boutique. I called Delia yesterday to warn—"

"Hold up. You what?" Gaze narrowed, he shook his head. "Please tell me you didn't tell her where you are."

"Of course, not. I wouldn't be that dumb." She

set down the green Sharpie she'd been using.

"Have you ever heard of a wiretap? Geez, Mais. Big mistake. *Huge*."

"How is it wrong to talk to a friend? I was scared for her. If she'd heard from Vicente, don't you think she'd have told me? What's wrong with you? Why do you always want to fight?"

He sighed. "What I want is to keep you safe. I can't do that if you talk to random people from your supposedly secret location."

"Dee isn't just *random* or *people*. She's a dear friend we've known since forever."

"Right. How could I forget you're an expert judge of character?"

"That was a low blow."

"Sorry." But it was the truth. He'd once loved that Maisey was trusting enough to have never met a soul she didn't consider an instant friend. Now? The safest route would be assuming the worst in everyone until they proved otherwise. Honestly, he'd been proud of her for second-guessing even Harding. Five million bucks was life-changing money. A lot of people would do a lot of bad things to get it. "Remember how nice Harvey and Mildred seemed? Folks are motivated by all kinds of things. Money is universal."

"What motivates you?"

"Excuse me?"

"What about my question don't you understand?" She leaned in. "Why are you going to all of this trouble for me? If it's not for money, then what?"

"It's my job."

"Liar. Your mom said you've been with her for a while and showed no signs of wanting to rejoin your team."

"We're not an official team anymore. Our SEAL days ended a long while back." He'd screwed that up, too.

"From what I can tell, you and your friends are still very much a team. Sure, you might be private contractors now instead of working for the government, but your end goals seem pretty much the same—keeping innocent people safe. Does that sound about right?"

"Stop. You don't know anything about me. We haven't really talked in years."

"Isn't that what we're doing now?"

"No. This is more like an interrog—"

"Yo, Nash." Jasper entered the kitchen. "Heads-up. We've got a guy out front claiming to be a door-to-door salesman. Everett and Briggs watched him work his way up the street, but we're not buying it. Want us to *detain* him?"

"No. If he is one of Vicente's guys that would tip them off that we're not a normal household. Once he's gone, we need to discreetly be on our way."

"Got it."

"Oh—and run a check on an old friend of ours, Delia Leti. She's here in Jacksonville. I want eyes and ears on her."

"Roger, that."

"We're leaving?" Maisey asked.

"Yes. ASAP. Pack up yourself and—"

While he'd been talking to Jasper, Maisey had lifted her son from his carrier and now rocked him in her arms.

"When are you giving that kid a name?"

"Why do you care?"

Nash stopped short of firing off a smart-assed answer. "Can we not do this? Bickering gives me a headache."

"You started it with your snide remark about my son's lack of a name. Don't you think I know he needs one? But at this point, he doesn't even have a birth certificate or social security number. Officially, he doesn't exist anywhere but on hospital records, the news, and my heart. What kind of twisted world did I bring him into? And now, we're going to be back on the run?"

"Look . . ." His every instinct told him to take her free hand, or draw her onto his lap so he could properly hold her and her baby. But if he gave himself permission to comfort her, what happened next? How did he show her how much he cared about not only her physical safety, but overall well-being, without allowing her further into his soul? Because the truth about why he felt so on edge had less to do with worries about her ex and his guys storming their temporary castle, than it did about Nash protecting his own aching heart. "You're going to be a great mom. Give the poor kid a name. Any name. Bob or Peter or Doug. I'll bet when you two settle into your new routine, you'll call him by some goofy nickname. Like maybe he'll eat too many saltine crackers and one day you'll teasingly call him Salty and it'll stick."

"Let me get this straight. You want me to call this precious child Bob or Salty?" Her faint smile caused all manner of chaos in his already tight chest.

"Those sound as good as any others. What are your top picks?"

"Mom likes the name Zane, but I think it's too harsh for a baby."

"He's not going to weigh six pounds forever."

She stuck out her tongue. "Thanks for that parenting tip."

"My pleasure."

"Your mom wants me to call him Richard."

"Nice. That was her father's name. What are you leaning toward?"

"Joseph—Joe for short. That was my grandfather's name."

"Perfect. So what's the problem?"

"That's just it. I do want it to be perfect. I've already failed by giving him an awful father. What if I mess up his name, too? He'll hate me before he even knows me."

"For all the grief you give me about holding on to my past, you're equally as bad. What happened with your ex is old news. Odds are, one of my guys will flush him out soon, and then we'll hand him over to police we know can't be bought."

"Didn't you tell me everyone has a price? How do you know your cops will be any different? Even if they do get Vicente behind bars, what's going to keep him there?" She rose and paced, cradling her son close. "How am I ever going to be truly free?"

"Have patience. We're working on it, okay?" Nash's arms ached from the effort of not pulling her into the sort of embrace that would allow her to not only feel secure in the moment, but in their shared future. Only that would be a lie. Because regardless of the outcome with her ex, because Nash's heart was already taken, the two of them could never be a couple again. "As long as there's breath in my body, I'll never give up."

"Thank you." Her sad, shimmering gaze made him all the more determined to return her smile.

"No problem." Only where she was concerned, everything was a problem. The faint scent of lilacs in her hair. Her full lower lip he remembered drawing into his mouth to keep her from crying out when they'd hidden in his bedroom closet to *study* each other. The longer they were together, the more memories flooded his system—not replacing those of his wife, but coming into clearer focus than they'd ever been before. They weren't all of hot sex, but Sunday dinners and yard work and riding bikes with her down to the corner store. Holding her when she'd sobbed over not making the debate team. Having her comfort him when he'd lost the state baseball title. Their lives had been tangled to the point that he wasn't sure where he left off and she began. He'd always assumed that was the way they would always be, then she'd rejected him and he'd walked away. Prior to losing his wife and baby, that was the most crushing pain he'd ever felt. Why had he ever given her that much power? "So is it official? You're naming the little guy, Joe?"

"Yes. I love it. Thank you."

He was the one owing her thanks. Her smile brought back the sun. More than anything, he wanted to hold her and kiss her and comb his hands through her soft curls, but how could he do any of that while honoring Hope?

"Should I go pack?"

"No time." Not wanting the intimacy that may stem from simply holding her hand, he pressed his palm to the small of her back, propelling her toward the garage.

"What about the baby's gear?"

"Grab his diaper bag, but that's it. I'll have one

of the guys bring the rest."

"Where are we even going?"

"I would tell you, but I'm afraid you'd blab."

"Shove it up your—"

Jasper cleared his throat. "Hate to break up this love fest, but I'm afraid I've got bad news about Delia Leti. She's dead."

25

Upon hearing Delia was dead, the only thing keeping Maisey upright was the fact that if she collapsed, her son could be hurt. There was a loud ringing in her ears and her pulse had gone haywire.

"Let's hustle," Nash slipped his arm around her shoulder, supporting her while helping her get to the SUV he'd parked in the four-car garage. "Jasper, in case we have more uninvited company, you follow. Once you radio back an all-clear, Harding can follow with our moms. The rest of the team can head out after that. We'll rendezvous at the appointed location at—" he glanced at a black digital watch "—thirteen hundred hours. Clear?"

"As a Texas sky." Jasper relayed all of the information via radio to the rest of the team while

Nash gingerly took the baby from Maisey's arms, got him fastened in his carseat, then helped her into the back to sit alongside him.

Nash steered the hulking vehicle from the neighborhood without incident, then veered onto the freeway.

Only once they'd left the city and Jasper was still within view, did Maisey dare ask the question she feared she already knew how Nash would answer. "Do you think Vicente killed Delia?"

He met her gaze in the rearview. "I think it's a given."

She crossed her arms, staring past the window through silent tears. When would this nightmare end? The day was bright and sunny—made for Florida tourists. Not running from a psycho killer. Why didn't the rest of the world see Vicente as she did? How could he have them all fooled?

She placed her hand on her son's chest. He blessedly had no idea what they were going through. Instead, he peered in wonder at the shining white dot on the ceiling that was caused by the sun's reflection in a side mirror.

"Relax. Judging by his profile, Vicente's not a patient man. We'll find him—I won't rest until he's locked away for good."

Maisey nodded, but didn't fully believe Nash's reassurance.

Up ahead, traffic had slowed to a stop.

"Do you think there was a wreck?" she asked.

"No telling." He radioed to Jasper to stay alert.

One by one, cars inched forward. On the raised, divided highway, there was nowhere else to go.

A muscle ticked in Nash's whisker-stubbled jaw. He tapped his index finger against the wheel.

"What's the matter?" she asked.

"I don't like this. One of the most critical roles in security is establishing two or three escape routes. Unless Harding sends a copter, we've pretty much got none."

A quick glance out her window showed what he meant. The shoulder was barely two feet wide. A twenty-foot drop to black water and thick vegetation waited on the other side. Ahead, stretched a double row of cars as far as the eye could see. Behind— same story.

"I can just make out police lights. I haven't seen construction signs, so there must be a wreck." He shifted in his seat, then lowered the A/C.

"Your body language says you don't think it's that simple."

He sighed before they shared a look in the rear-view.

"A few weeks ago," she said, "I wouldn't have believed Vicente capable of pulling a stunt like shutting down a freeway. Now, judging by the way he bribed an entire police department, then managed to make the whole state believe he's the victim, anything's possible."

"Exactly, which is why if there's even a hint of this turning bad, I'm going to need you to be incredibly brave."

"Oh no—I'm not leaping into that swamp with my baby."

"I'm not asking you to." They'd moved up a dozen car lengths, and now had a clear sight line to a police road block. Was this an ordinary drunk driver check, or something more? "There's only a Jeep Wrangler between us and Jasper's Hummer."

"I thought it was Harding's?"

"Semantics. He's behind the wheel."

"What's with you guys and your giant cars?"

"Bulletproof and big are always good when under attack."

Made sense. At the word *attack*, her stomach cramped. How often did he face gunfire?

"Focus. Right now, take Joe from his carrier and hold him. Unbuckle the seat, and stash it in back—any other baby paraphernalia, too."

"I'm afraid to ask why." But she followed his instructions.

"In a few minutes, you're going to open the back door and slip out in as small a space as possible, then duck to the ground and crawl beneath the car behind us until you get to Jasper's. There's an escape hatch beneath it, but in this case, I want you to open the door and climb up into his vehicle. He'll help. You'll be in an airtight box that has its own ventilation system good for twenty-four hours if necessary."

"Wait—*what*?" All of this was sounding very James Bond.

"You can do it. Go, Mais. Now."

"But—"

"*Now.*"

Forced into action, heart hammering in her ears, she hid all the baby gear in the back, then slipped from his SUV's safe, cool interior to suffocating heat.

Praying no one had seen her, she followed Nash's instructions to the letter in ducking beneath their vehicle, then scrambling onto her back, inching between the tires to the Jeep with her precious son hitching a ride on her chest.

Her eyes stung from the heat and exhaust. Concrete bit the tender skin of her palms as she used them to help scoot on her back. Terror didn't begin to describe the nerves making her every muscle scream, but for little Joe, she clamped her lips tight and pushed through. Time fractured and seconds ticked by like hours. She'd made it midway down the length of the vehicle behind Nash's SUV when it moved.

She froze.

26

Nash struggled for his next thought, let alone breath.

He was two cars from the cops who'd blocked both lanes, funneling all vehicles into a single lane of passage. It was now clear that all vehicles were being checked for a specific element—what that was, he didn't know.

He slipped on mirrored Ray-Bans and a Florida Gators ball cap.

If these cops were legit, they could be on the hunt for an escaped convict or this could be as routine as an insurance check—both of which seemed unlikely given their current location. Which made the likelihood of this event being attached to Vicente all the greater.

Given Delia's death, he surmised that Maisey's bestie ratted her out for a fee by agreeing to have her phone tapped. Vicente, in turn, had his men case the safe house's neighborhood, and possibly even trailed them onto the highway, but then lost them. With thirty-five miles before the next exit, if Vicente had radioed ahead to still more of his men to be on the look-out, this would be a brilliant trap.

As much as Nash hated to admit it, the bastard was one hell of an opponent.

"Any sign of her?" he asked into the radio shared with Jasper.

"Not yet, but I've got this."

"You'd better, man. Maisey and her son mean . . ." *Everything.* If something happened to her, he wasn't sure what he'd do, so his plan was to make damned sure her and Joe came out of this healthy and happy. As for his own state of mind? He'd worry about it later. "Well, they're important."

"I get it."

"Shit, we're moving. See her?"

"Yeah. She's frozen. Hold up, and I'll get in position over her."

The next twenty seconds felt like a lifetime. Nash would have said his whole life flashed before his eyes, but in that instant, he didn't see merely his life, but combined moments with the girl next door who'd shared most every occasion with him. Christmases and Thanksgivings. Graduations and birthdays. Highs and lows. He'd loved Hope, but hadn't realized the true depth of what he'd shared with his Maisey. And she was *his*—would always be.

Maybe if only in a secret corner of his heart.

His pulse raged in his ears. Waiting was torture.

The stunt he'd asked Maisey to perform would have been no big deal for him or any of the guys on his team, but for a woman who'd just had a baby— while carrying that baby—all he could do was pray it hadn't been too much.

The guy in the Jeep honked, jolting him from his thoughts.

"Got her," Jasper said over the radio. "Mother and son are secure."

"Thanks, man." Nash took a minute before pulling forward to compose himself and even his erratic breaths. "It's showtime."

He pulled alongside the uniformed officers who had parked their squad cars at a diagonal across the bridge. None of this was normal. No way could he see a legit unit pulling an operation like this unless under the most dire circumstances.

Nash rolled down his window. "Afternoon, officers. What's the hold up?"

"Pardon the delay, but we've had word that a kidnapper may be heading this way. As a courtesy, we're checking all vehicles for the infant. Are you driving alone?"

"Yessir."

"Where you headed?" While the short, pock-marked man asked questions, a tallish guy with a shaved head scoped out Nash's vehicle.

"Pensacola. My wife and kids are over there, staying with her mother."

"She doesn't have a car to drive back on her own?"

Bald Guy walked around to the back.

"Is there a problem?" Nash asked.

"Not at all. Just making conversation." Easy smile. "Mind removing your hat and sunglasses?"

In the side mirror, Nash noticed Bald Guy talking to the driver of the Jeep behind him. The driver gestured to the passenger side of Nash's SUV, then shrugged.

"Sir? Sunglasses?"

"I recently had my eyes dilated, so if you don't mind, I'll keep them on." He did remove his hat, then mussed his hair so that it looked nothing like the straight-laced military pic showing on the nightly news.

Shit. The driver behind him was still animatedly chatting with Bald Guy. Had he seen Maisey's escape?

"Am I good to go?" Despite being unable to hear his voice over his pulse, Nash strove for a casual tone. Maisey and baby Joe were safely hidden. Logically, there was no way this could go wrong. Too bad Vicente had an uncanny knack for defying logic.

197

"My wife and kids are expecting me."

The driver of a Pizza Hut truck further back in the line honked, then leaned out his window. "Hey! What's the hold-up?"

"Yeah, you're good." The officer waved Nash through.

Nash checked his rearview to find Bald Guy chatting up Jasper.

In the whole time they'd been waiting, the police duo had never talked to more than one driver at a time. Why now?

"I said you're good to go." The officer double-tapped Nash's door.

While keeping an eye on Jasper in the rearview, Nash eased down on his gas pedal. If Jasper was in trouble, he didn't want to get too far. On the other hand, now that he had a clear escape, he wanted to be able to use it the second Jasper broke free.

Out of sight from the roadblock, since no additional cars had been allowed to pass, Nash pulled to the side.

What could be taking so long? The Jeep should have at least moved into view.

"Nash, copy?"

"I'm here. What's wrong?"

"We've got—"

Nash heard a gunshot's pop, then a squelch of feedback before the line went dead.

27

From inside her black-carpeted, coffin-shaped box, Maisey barely made out what sounded like a firecracker's *pop*, then muffled screams.

Had that been a gunshot?

Panic set in, or maybe it had never left from her harrowing trek between vehicles. In eerie green light, she tried slowing her breathing, but it was no good. Short and choppy was the best she could do. She tried rolling onto her side, but the turn was awkward while holding Joe.

Her throat ached from the effort of holding back tears and though a fan's reassuring drone assured her she had adequate air, her caged lungs failed to believe there could ever be enough.

Where is she? A man she didn't recognize shouted.

Who? Jasper asked. *I don't know what you're talking about.*

Get out.

No.

Maybe this will encourage you to listen?

What was the man doing? Holding a gun to Jasper's head? Her mind's eye conjured far more frightening images than could have possibly played out in the Hummer's front seat—at least she prayed the worst wasn't truly happening.

What the hell, man? What's your badge number? I'm turning you in for police brutality and harassment.

My badge number is Smith and Wesson. Where's the girl?

I already told you, I don't know.

Another pop. This one close enough to make Maisey's ears ring.

To keep from crying, she clamped her hand over her mouth.

But then the baby released a few fitful cries, and she was flipping him onto his belly, pressing his sweet face between her breasts. She whispered, "I'm sorry, sweetheart."

What was that?

What? Geez, you're psycho.

Get out of the vehicle. I'm not fooling around.

Good, because neither am I.

Another pop sounded, then the engine revved.

Stop him!

Pop, pop, pop.

Maisey bit her lip to keep from crying out. But then she was flung back by the sudden forward momentum. Feet braced against the box's lowest edge, she held Joe tight while gripping a metal bar mounted on the box's side.

Joe bawled.

"It's all right," she assured, even though he had every reason to cry.

Eyes squeezed shut, her mind's eye saw Nash. He'd promised not to let anyone hurt her, and she believed him.

Somehow, someway, he'd make good on his promise to see her safely through to the end of Vicente's twisted power game.

When this was over, she'd apologize to him for her previous selfish attitude. Of course, he missed his wife. He wouldn't be the man Maisey had always loved if he hadn't.

When the vehicle's motion evened out, she calmed herself and her son. "I'm sorry, sweetie. Once we're safe, we're going to have an epic cuddle session. Maybe we'll even convince Nash to join in?"

However long he needed to feel right about being with her, Maisey would wait. She'd been responsible for them ever having broken up in the first place. The least she could do was give him the space he now needed.

Her breathing had almost returned to normal when she heard more pops—only this time, in a machine gun's rapid fire.

28

When jasper had for all practical purposes shoved the Jeep out of his way, since he'd backtracked, Nash had a front row view.

Had Maisey and her baby not been in the car, he might have applauded Jasper's bold escape, but with so much at stake, he'd damned near bit through his tongue. He made a U-turn, then waited for the Hummer to pass before assuming the backup position to fend off the inevitable repercussions.

Jasper pitched a destroyed radio from his window before flashing Nash a cocky grin and thumbs-up. Had Vicente's goons shot it?

Nash wished he felt more positive about the afternoon's events, especially when Vicente's guys—no way were they actual cops—flipped on their lights and sirens to give chase.

Jasper set the pace at one-twenty on the lonely stretch of road.

The scammy cops easily followed in a single car with the bald guy popping off shots out his window.

Considering the odds of the goon actually hitting any target at that speed, Nash wasn't too concerned until his adversaries pulled out a freaking submachine gun. One or more shots connected with the rear window and the glass shattered.

Swell . . .

At their high speed, they'd caught up with traffic, and were forced to slow in order to safely zig and zag between mini-vans crammed with kids. Traveling salesmen and massive tractor trailer rigs. In that instant, never had Nash hated a man more than Vicente. What was the point of any of this?

Assuming Vicente's ultimate goal was to get his hands on his son, he sure had a funny way of accomplishing the task. Did the idiot realize how much danger he was landing his little guy in? Did he care? Or was this all about control? Proving he was the bigger man?

Endless miles later, Jasper took the first exit they came to.

Nash followed.

Oddly enough, Vicente's bogus cops did not.

What was that about?

Jasper drove ten miles back from the freeway

until reaching a combo gas station and convenience store.

By the time Nash parked his ride and killed the engine, he trembled to such a degree he was afraid he might not be able to walk.

Maisey and the baby stood alongside the Hummer. *Safe.*

When he'd thought those guys would get past him to unleash their fury on Maisey and her son and his best friend, Jasper, pure panic had set in.

"Nash! You're alright." Clutching her baby, Maisey ran to him, and he hugged her close, burying his face in her hair, breathing in her lilac scent. "I was so scared."

He tightened his hold until Joe squirmed between them.

"Sorry, fella." Nash backed away.

"He's okay," Maisey said. "Thanks to Jasper, we're both fine." She hugged Nash's friend, then stood on her tiptoes to kiss his cheek.

Jasper reddened, then held up his hands, teasing, "Back off the merchandise. Wanna get me shot by your glaring man?"

"My man, huh?" Maisey beamed. "I like the sound of that."

Nash didn't. He was beyond relieved she and the baby were safe, but that didn't mean this nightmare was over. "Hate to be the bearer of bad news, but does anyone else find it strange how easily Vicente's men backed off? Almost as if they were—"

"Leading you into a trap?" Vicente, dressed in a white linen suit with a yellow tie and matching pocket square, stepped out from around the back of the shabby building. "Bravo. I do love a worthy adversary."

Nash had been too intent on seeing Maisey to have noticed the tail-end of a black limo stretching out from behind the seedy, cement-block structure.

"And Maisey . . ." He held out his arms. A diamond-drenched watch sparked in the blazing sun. "It seems like a lifetime since I last saw you. And now, you've gifted me with my son. How can I ever thank you?"

"Let us go, Vicente. End the senseless killing. You didn't need to kill Delia."

"Was that her name? I'll start a scholarship program in her honor."

Nash clenched his teeth while Vicente fingered one of Maisey's curls, then skimmed his fingertips over the crown of little Joe's head. Nash would have lunged for the monster's throat, but five men trailed their boss. All held their guns on Maisey.

"She was a beauty, but nowhere near as lovely as you."

Maisey spit on him.

He calmly took a white handkerchief from the chest pocket of his coat and wiped his cheek clean. "Interesting story—my wife makes these hankies for me by the dozens. She comes from a highly traditional family. Her mother made her father's handkerchiefs and it means the world to her to continue that tradition in our marriage."

"You're sick," Maisey said. "How can you talk about your wife, knowing what you've done to me?"

"Oh, darling, everything we did was with my wife's approval. In fact, she helped me pick you, and even suggested ways to best woo you. Since she is not able to carry my child, she decided a surrogate was the next best thing. But now that our son is safely in the world, she'd prefer you exit . . ." He grasped her forearm, guiding her toward his car.

"Slow down," Nash grasped Maisey's free arm. "She's not going anywhere with you. Neither is her son."

"Gentlemen . . ." He nodded to his goon squad who had slowly circled. "Since we may have an audience, please dispose of them in a discreet manner."

Before Nash could even reach for his Glock, two meatheads with faces only a bulldog's mom could love surged toward him, while another grabbed his wrists from behind.

Jasper wasn't faring much better.

"Nash?" Maisey struggled against Vicente's hold, but could only do so much while still holding her baby.

"I've got this. Just don't get into his car." For an instant, Nash went limp in his attacker's arms, then grabbed his wrist to position himself behind him, jerking back on his arm with enough force to hear a satisfying crunch of bone against tendon.

Maisey screamed.

Vicente stepped back to allow another of his men to cover her mouth, and yet another to man-handle her into the now running limo.

Nash fought his way past his current attacker with a well-placed fist to his ugly face.

"You good?" he shouted to Jasper.

"Yeah! Go after your girl!"

"Roger, that." Nash reached the limo just as the driver pulled away. He lunged for the back door's handle, but was too late.

Not caring who saw—in fact, the more witness-es, the better, he took his Glock from his holster, spread his legs to give himself a more stable shot, then *bam*, *bam*, *bam*, blew out both rear tires.

The vehicle fishtailed on the gravel lot, raising a dust cloud through which Nash could hardly see. When the dust settled, and the vehicle was still mov-ing, he shot again, taking out the driver's side front tire, as well.

The thug behind the wheel was good, but not good enough to keep forward momentum on his side with three shredded tires and rims sinking into soft gravel.

From inside the car came the sound of the baby crying.

Behind Nash, a plaid-wearing good ol' boy emerged from the store with a few hefty friends. "We don't want trouble. Y'all best be on your way."

"That guy in the limo . . ." Nash never took his eyes from the rear window. "He's got my wife and child." Up until that very second, Nash had been determined to hold tight to Hope's memory, but sadly, he realized that's all she now was. That didn't mean he loved her any less, but that Maisey and Joe needed—*deserved*—all of him, all the time. Not only the parts he felt emotionally equipped to handle. If they all made it through the next few minutes alive, they'd have the rest of their lives to figure out a happy ending—assuming this time when he proposed, Maisey accepted.

"Wait a minute . . ." the store clerk said from behind him. "Are you the folks we've been seeing on the news? If so, don't that mean there's five million reasons for me to believe you do intend to do that little woman and her baby harm?"

29

"Let me and my baby go, vicente. *Please.* It's over. I'm sure police are on their way. You can't win."

His leering smile made Maisey nauseous. "When are you going to learn, my pet, I *always* win."

"Come on out of there." There was a rap on the window. "Give me my five million, and I'll give you your man."

A satisfied groan spilled from Vicente's lips. "I do so love this country. People will do anything for a quick buck." He nodded to the grim-faced member of his security detail. "Off them all, then find a set of keys to match any vehicle. I'm excited to present our son to my wife. Ready the jet to leave within the hour."

"Vicente, no! Those men have done nothing to you. What if they have families?"

He rolled his eyes before trailing his associate, and leaving her alone in the car.

With each bullet's pop, Maisey died inside, fearing one targeted Nash. She needed to go to him, but she also needed to keep her son safe. What should she do? Her limbs had turned cold and sluggish with fear. She couldn't focus her eyes. Her gaze narrowed and her peripheral vision blurred. Terror lodged in the back of her throat, making it impossible to speak or scream or do anything other than grasp her wailing son.

"I'm sorry," she whispered, lurching with each new shot.

There were masculine shouts and obscenities and more shots fired than she could count.

Eyes closed, she wished herself anywhere but here—back to a time when she and Nash had been one. Why had she been foolish enough to throw him away?

The trapped air grew stifling in the heat.

With bullets flying, the last thing Maisey wanted to do was open the door, but unless she wanted her son or herself to pass from heatstroke, she needed to escape.

Holding tight to Joe, she opened the door facing the two-lane road, breathing deeply of the somewhat cooler air.

Cradling her son, she swung around to find Nash and Jasper both engaged in fist fights. She counted at least six dead men that the pair of SEALs must have eliminated. The men working the convenience store were gone, too, but their blood was on Vicente. Bile rose in the back of her throat. She struggled not to retch.

Vicente tried running for the limo, but Nash gave chase.

The two men exchanged more blows until Vicente drew a gun from a previously hidden chest holster.

Nash kicked the gun from his hand.

Nash and Vicente exchanged blow after blow. Nash's nose bled, and one eye had nearly swollen shut. Still, he kept pounding her ex like a machine.

Vicente got in a left hook, but then eventually sunk to his knees.

Jasper finished off his man, and pulled his cell phone from a side pocket of his desert-camo cargo pants.

"I so want to finish you here," Nash said to Vicente from between gritted teeth.

Maisey wanted the same, but not potentially at the risk of Nash's freedom. He was hurt bad enough and needed rest. Even Vicente couldn't escape what he'd now done.

"You don't have the spine to do the job." Barely upright, Vicente took a swing at Nash, but hit only air.

"Funny . . ." Nash spit out a mouthful of blood. "But it seems to me you're the one on the ground. Maybe you should try being a little nicer?"

"Nash, leave him alone!" Maisey pleaded. "He's like poking a snake. Let the police handle it from here."

"What I'll be," her ex said, "is the man who sends you to hell."

"Screw you." Nash drew his gun, pointing the business end at Vicente's head.

"Cavalry's on the way," Jasper said. "Want me to zip-tie him all nice and pretty for the cops?"

"Sure." Nash used his forearm to wipe blood from his nose and chin. "Thanks."

"My pleasure."

Maisey wasn't sure whether to run to Nash or wait for him to come to her. Had the danger finally passed? Was it safe to breathe?

Poor little Joe hadn't gotten the memo. He cried all the harder.

"Shh . . ." She gave him a light jiggle. "Everything's going to be okay."

"*Perra*!" Vicente shouted. "If my wife and I can't have my son, no one will."

In fractions of a second, Maisey helplessly watched as Vicente leapt up to take Jasper's gun. Before she could scream, he aimed it at Joe and fired, only her baby wasn't hit.

Nash had flung himself in front of her and Joe, and now, he shot Vicente in his chest before collapsing to the sun-bleached gravel in a pool of his own deep, red blood.

Maisey cried out, running to Nash, who'd been shot.

Jasper was back on his phone.

Everything slowed. She tried getting to Nash, but her limbs felt as weak as if she were made of pudding. She was conscious that she was screaming, but couldn't make out her own words.

Why was this happening? Hadn't what Vicente already put both of them through been enough? Why was she now having to face losing Nash for a second, agonizingly more permanent time?

"Don't you leave me," she said on the heels of a sob. She'd crumpled alongside him, holding her son in the crook of her arm, pulling Nash's head onto her lap, pressing Joe's blanket to his chest wound, whispering words of love.

He was eerily still. His breaths were shallow.

"Nash, I love you. Please stay with me—however you want. If you can only be friends, that's enough. But I don't ever want to be separated from you again."

Jasper grasped Nash's wrist, checking his pulse.

"Strong. He'll fight through." Nash's friend cupped his hand to her shoulder for a reassuring squeeze. "Plus, Harding's got a medical helicopter already headed this way."

"Thank you," Maisey said. "For everything. We wouldn't have made it without you."

Jasper shrugged. "You're welcome, but it was no biggie. All in a day's work."

"Yeah, well, you're both crazy."

"True . . ." Jasper grinned. "But at least we're also damned good looking."

How he could joke at a time like this was beyond her, but she cast him a faint smile and nodded, but kept pressing the blanket to Nash's wound.

Ten feet away, Vicente's corpse gazed at her with a blank stare.

Maisey thought she'd be happy when he was finally gone, but seeing him dead brought no joy, only a strong sense of resolve to do something special with the rest of her life.

30

Hours later, maisey woke from a light sleep to find Nash still resting comfortably in a Jacksonville hospital. He'd lost a lot of blood, but the bullet had miraculously missed vital organs and lodged itself in a rib. Doctors removed it, and he was expected to make a full recovery.

Harding and Jasper were handling the mountain of police paperwork, leaving Nash free to heal.

With the threat of danger behind them, Maisey had left Joe with her mom, so she could be with Nash when he woke. Her son had been so distraught by the gunfire that it had taken most of the afternoon to calm him. Her mom's last report was that he'd finally succumbed to sleep.

Aside from the oxygen's faint gurgle, the room

was tomb silent.

Which made her nervous.

She rose, standing at Nash's bedside to make sure he was well and truly okay. His chest regularly rose and fell, and his eye was already looking better. In the heat of this war—and that's what her ultimate escape from Vicente had been—she'd dreamed of spending the rest of her life with Nash. But now that the crisis had passed, she feared that dream could never be a reality.

It still didn't seem real—that Vicente was gone. That she and her son's lives were now forever worry free. But she would worry—not about herself, but for this man who carried a burden so heavy he might never rest.

She drew a chair to his bedside and lowered the rail. Sitting, she leaned forward, resting her cheek on the back of his hand.

"How can I ever thank you for saving me?" She stroked the hair on his tanned forearm. "I don't like thinking of myself as a damsel in distress, but you certainly played the role of my knight in shining armor. You always have, you know? Whether it was saving me from a playground bully or helping me cram for finals or fill out college scholarship applications, you were always there—until you weren't. And I did that. I know. I ended us. As bad as that hurts, I know for both of our sakes that I need to let you go and move on. Our time together has been scary and exhausting and at times a bit of a rush, but you were doing a job, and I read far too much into your protector role. You weren't—"

"Geez . . . What's a guy gotta do to get sleep around here?"

"You're awake?"

"I'm talking, aren't I?" He shifted his hand out from under her to cup her cheek. "You're beautiful. Like, crazy, stupid take-my-breath-away gorgeous."

"Nash, I—"

"Shh." He planted his finger over her lips. "You had your say, but now it's my turn to talk."

"You heard all of that and didn't stop me?" Mortified didn't begin to cover how that revelation made her feel. What she'd said had been private—meant for the version of him she'd forever carry in her private heart—not the real deal.

"Ever think I might have a few secrets to spill?"

Teary eyed, she shook her head.

"When your psycho ex shot me, all I could do was pray I stayed alive long enough to tell you how much I love you."

"As a close friend?"

"Do you have to keep interrupting?"

"Sorry. Nervous habit." She pretended to zip her lips, lock them, then toss the imaginary key.

"Since odds are you have every intention of butting in again, I'm going to make this quick. There's nothing friendly or brotherly about what I feel for you. It's hot and achy and makes me want to drag you into this bed and do things that would sky-rocket my pulse. Make no mistake, I genuinely loved Hope. She taught me to be a better, kinder, more patient man. What I didn't understand before almost losing you was that loving you isn't replacing her, it's honoring her by opening my heart to its full capacity to let you back in. If you'll have me, I can't wait to be a husband to you and father to Joe. I want to kill spiders for you and mow the lawn and weed the gar-den. I want us to host holiday dinners for our moms and play board games and do puzzles on rainy days. I want the kind of life we talked about sharing back when we were kids and didn't fully appreciate how precious that kind of normalcy would truly be. I want—"

"How about what I want?" She hated to yet again interrupt, but this couldn't wait.

He scowled. "Are you turning down my pro-posal again?"

"As if . . ." She stood, leaning over him to re-move the oxygen tubes from his nose. "All of what you said sounds great, but I'm capable of killing my own spiders, and at the moment, what I want seems more urgent than a game of Scrabble."

"I don't know . . . Scrabble can get pretty in-tense."

"Now, who's talking too much?" She leaned closer and closer until his warm, familiar breath fanned her upper lip, making her tingle with the kinds of needs that would sadly have to wait until they were both off medical abstinence.

Finally, *finally*, she touched her lips to his and happily groaned. Their kiss was everything she'd remembered and craved.

At least until he pulled back. "Maisey?"

"Yes?"

"I just thought of a major problem."

She tensed. "If you're about to tell me you changed your mind about us—"

He kissed her quiet. "Relax. All I wanted to say is that at some point soon, we're gonna have to make a return trip to the Everglades to fetch my truck."

EPILOGUE

"**H**on, I'm telling you that food network chef said this is the best way to get our turkey extra juicy. He said if we don't cook it on super low heat, starting ridiculously early in the morning, it will never be done in time for guests." It was their first Thanksgiving as husband and wife, and Nash's friends wouldn't stop giving him grief about his new penchant for cooking. But then what did he care? In a few hours, they could all eat crow instead of his delicious bird. His meal would hands down be the best any of those bozos had ever tasted.

Maisey yawned. "As far as I'm concerned, there's only one thing delicious enough to wake me this early on a day off." She'd taken a loan to buy her old shop from Delia's parents, and sales had been great but her schedule hectic.

"Oh yeah? What's that?" He added a final sprig of fresh rosemary to his crowning Thanksgiving glory, then placed the lid on the new roasting pan and put the bird in the oven.

"I think you know." She hefted herself onto the granite counter of the newly-renovated three-bedroom ranch they'd bought on the same block as their two moms. At times, it was too close for comfort, but it sure came in handy when they needed a sitter. "All this food porn you've been making me watch has me hungry for something meatier than gravy."

"Yeah?" He washed his hands and dried them on a dishcloth before crossing to her, easing his hands under her lush curls, then kissing her, drinking her in, loving her with every breath of his being.

She'd slept in one of the white button-downs Harding forced him to wear when he met clients at Trident, Inc.'s new Jacksonville office. He hated those shirts, but loved seeing them on his sexy wife.

Even better? He loved taking them off of her. One by one, he unfastened buttons, kissing a trail along the way. He pressed his lips to her collarbone, to each breast, to her abdomen, and then lower to the sweet spot between her legs. He urged her legs open and flattened his hand against her chest, nudging her back against the upper cabinet.

He found her clit, laving it with his tongue until

she cried out and pulled his hair. Since they were already trying to give Joe a baby brother or sister, Nash didn't bother with a condom, but eased inside while tugging her nearer the counter's edge.

She wrapped her arms around him, pressing open-mouthed kisses to his neck. "I love you . . . I love you . . . I love you."

"I love you," he said on the heels of a moan. "I love you so damned much. Think our mothers would frown if when we all say what we're thankful for, I admit that I'm damned thankful for my wife's sexy—"

The house phone rang.

"Talk about being saved by the bell. First—who would be calling this early on Thanksgiving? Second—no, you can't say anything about our sex lives at the dinner table. Third—don't you dare stop until . . . *Yes, yes* . . ."

The ringing quit long enough for Nash to spill his seed deep inside her, then indulge in a nice, long make-out session before it started up again. "Want me to get it? Or should we go straight for another round?"

"You should probably at least see who it is." She shrugged the open halves of his shirt back over her shoulders. "It might be one of our moms."

He sighed, then picked up the phone. "Jasper. What the hell, man? I haven't even found the coffee, let alone made a cup."

"Sorry, man. I'm calling everyone. Remember that girl I met? Eden?"

"Yeah." Nash scratched his head. "Thought she was in Iceland."

"Antarctica."

"Same difference—sort of."

"Stop screwing around, she's in trouble."

"What's up?" Nash's stomach tensed with adrenaline. He hadn't been a key member of any protection team since getting out of the hospital. As much as he loved playing homemaker, he was itching to get back to action—even if that meant working the home office while part of the team was gone.

"Mind if we all meet at your place in an hour? She left a cryptic message I want all of you to hear."

"Sure. Head over. Maisey won't mind."

She raised her eyebrows and frowned. "If this is about football . . ."

Nash shook his head, then ended the call.

"Everything okay?"

After one more lingering kiss, he said, "We're about to find out."

Dear Reader—

I can't thank you enough for spending time with Nash and Maisey. All of my characters are dear to me, but these two sometimes made me cry, scream, laugh or all of the above! LOL! If you enjoyed their story, pretty please with-a-cherry-on-top leave a review on the site where you purchased it.

The next book in my SEAL Team: Disavowed series, OUTCAST, features Eden and Jasper. These two damaged souls have some awfully big secrets that play out in the midst of a deadly, Antarctic-based treasure hunt that I hope you'll devour! I've included the first chapter for a sneak peek . . .

Happy Reading—Laura Marie

OUTCAST

SEAL Team: Disavowed Book 2

1

"They're all dead . . ." English lit professor, Eden Marabella, dropped the satellite phone she'd been speaking into. It shattered against the rocks at her feet, but shock at the sight before her made the loss of their team's primary outside communication tool a non-issue.

Her throat closed with emotion, and her eyes stung.

The more of the grisly scene she digested, the more her stomach roiled.

She retched at the sheer amount of blood spilled across the ice. It had frozen in pools beneath the majestic creatures, standing in stark contrast to the Orcas' beautiful black and white markings.

Her father's associate, Dane Northrup, a marine biologist from Stony Brook University in New York, slipped his arm around her shoulders, comforting her through her latest round of nausea. "Deep breaths," he coached. "Ride it out."

"W-what happened?" she asked, her voice shallow and dazed. "It looks like an entire pod." Dozens upon dozens of the killer whales had washed upon the snow and ice-crusted shore of their stretch of Antarctica's Ross Sea. Her father, a marine biology professor from the University of Tampa had been coming here for years. He and his students had raised millions for conservation and research, and now had a private station manned year-round with students and professors pursuing independent studies.

Her poor father silently moved among the beached creatures as if under a dark spell. His shoulders slumped. Silent tears glistened on his ruddy cheeks in the bright November sun. The day was a rare jewel with the temperature almost above freezing and the horizon clear. Tragedy didn't happen on afternoons like this, so why were they facing so much death now?

Early that morning, Eden and her dad had

caught a ride with friends stationed at McMurdo. Dane followed with two students who'd opted to stay in their rooms to get settled.

The walk to the beach had become an annual tradition for Eden and her father. One typically highlighted by visiting an Adélie penguin colony on the rocky point. In the shock over the orcas, she'd forgotten them. She was now afraid to glance in that direction.

"Dane," she turned to him, selfishly wishing he were Jasper, the sweetheart she'd been dating back in Denver. She'd been on the sat phone leaving a heart-felt message for him, trying to explain the impossible as to why she'd broken things off, when she'd crested the last rise on the shore trail to witness the carnage-filled view. "Could you please check the penguins? I can't . . ."

"Eden, I'm sorry, but—"

"How did this happen?" Her sob cut off his words. The instant she'd heard his apology, she'd made the mistake of looking for herself.

The penguins were dead, too.

Dane grasped her upper arms to keep her from collapsing onto her knees. "I promise we'll get to the bottom of this. I won't rest till we have an answer to why."

She nodded.

When he wrapped his arms around her for a hug, it only reminded her how much she missed Jasper. Until now, she hadn't realized how great a role he'd played in her life—not that it mattered.

She'd never see him again.

She wasn't even sure why she'd called, other than that she loved this place more than any other in the world. On what would no doubt be her last visit, she'd wanted to share it with him.

That said, at the moment, the man who needed her most was her grief-stricken father who wept over the still penguin chick he cradled in his palms.

Eden had set out in his direction when the ground began to shake . . .

Ready for more?
Eden and Jasper's story, OUTCAST,
is available now.

ABOUT THE AUTHOR

Laura Marie Altom is the author of fifty novels. Her award-winning work has appeared on numerous bestseller lists and worldwide, she has over a million books in print. Laura lives in Tulsa, Oklahoma with her husband of twenty-five years. This former teacher has been blessed with boy/girl twins and a menagerie of dogs and cats. For fun, Laura's content to garden, thrift-shop or curl up with a great book.

Laura loves hearing from readers, and can be reached at the following social media outlets:

E-mail balipalm@aol.com
Website: www.lauramariealtom.com
Facebook: www.facebook.com/LauraMarieAltom
Twitter: @LauraMarieAltom
Instagram: www.instagram.com/lauramariealtom
Pinterest: www.pinterest.com/lauramariealtom